TORI MARTIN

The Summer of Us

To all the kids fighting cancer.

Contents

IV   August

V   September

VI   October

Preface

Riley's first memory was from when he was a little over two and a half. Most people don't have memories from that early, but Riley's only explanation was that it was one of the most monumental happenings in his life, and that's why he remembered.

He was sitting on Mamie's lap on the couch in the lounge, listening to her read him a bunny rabbit story. He couldn't remember any other details from then– what he was wearing, or exactly where on the couch he was sitting– but he did remember the story she was reading to him. Mom and Dad were at the hospital, and while he didn't really understand why, it had something to do with the fact that Mom's stomach had gotten really big lately, and he was going to maybe get a little brother or sister. He was really excited about that. His friend Ben had just gotten a little sister, Ellie, and Riley had held her at church the other Sunday. Ellie was so soft and warm and cuddly.

The front door opened with a squeak, and Riley jumped off Mamie's lap. He ran down the hall to the front door.

"Mommy! Daddy!" he cried. He skidded to a stop in front of them. They each held a car seat.

"Did you both bring me a baby?" he asked, confused.

Mommy laughed happily. "Riley, you have two little sisters! Mommy had twins!"

Daddy set his car seat down and pulled back the blanket. Riley knelt down beside it. A tiny little human, wrapped in a cream blanket, slept soundly in the seat. Riley reached out and touched her cheek. It was as soft as a flower petal. A wisp of brown hair curled across the tiny forehead.

"That's your sister Taylor," Daddy said. Then he pulled down the pink blanket on the other car seat. "And this is Mackenzie."

"Ri-ri hold dem?" Riley asked.

"Sure, let's go sit down on the couch; then you can hold them." Riley scampered to the lounge. Mamie had discreetly left, so the little family could enjoy the moment together, and the bunny rabbit book lay discarded on the arm rest. Riley climbed up on the couch and held his arms out eagerly.

Daddy put the cream coloured bundle in his arms, and positioned a pillow behind the baby's head.

"Tay-tay?" Riley asked, recognizing the blanket.

"That's right," Mommy said, sitting down beside him with the pink bundle. Riley gave his baby sister a gentle squeeze and kissed her forehead.

"Tay-tay," he crooned softly. "I's you're big brudder."

Riley sighed and shook the memories out of his head. He turned back to the small frames on the hospital beds on either side of him. On his left, Taylor was curled up, her eyes squished tight against the pain. On the right, Mackenzie was fast asleep from the pain meds they had given her.

If only he could somehow rewrite history, and take back those two little baby girls. If only he could brush a magic wand over their futures and take out the pain and stress and sickness that spelled 'leukemia'.

"God, just please heal them. Please make them better again," he prayed.

Far away, somewhere down the hall in the oncology department, the faint ringing of a bell sounded. The sound of that bell would stay in his mind for weeks.

I

May

And so the journey begins.

1

Chapter 1

It's not every day that you get to walk down a long hallway, surrounded on either side by clapping nurses, to ring the bell. It's not every day that you get to do it with your sister, twin, and best friend, either.

Mackenzie and I have been through the worst and the best together. As identical twins, I guess if one gets cancer, the other one does, too; at least in our case.

But now the long days of pain and sickness, lying in two adjoining beds, are over.

I adjust my pink cowboy hat and grip Mackenzie's hand even tighter as we reach the bell.

Mom, Dad, and even Riley are crying as we take turns ringing the bell and signing our names on the wall. We are in remission.

○○ ○○ ○○ ○○ ○○

It's hard being fourteen and bald, but Mackenzie and I made a pact to make the most of it. We already have over twenty hats, headbands, and wigs collected between the two of us. We call it 'our hairy collection'.

Today is Thursday. On Monday we'll go back to school for the first time in, well, months. It's May and there are only two weeks left of school, but we want to say, "Hi," to our friends a little bit before summer hits.

I fall asleep on the hour-long drive to our ranch from the children's hospital in New Orleans. Mackenzie is slumped against the window in the seat beside me. Riley wakes me up as we pull into the long, tree-lined lane leading to Golden Creek Ranch.

The leafy green oaks bend over the lane, creating an emerald tunnel. It's hard to believe it's almost summer already.

We turn around the bend in the lane, and up ahead I can see the house with its white, stone colonnades and two story wrap-around porches. Giant leafy ferns sit exactly five feet apart along the porches. It still looks the same, and that brings me a sweet sense of relief.

It's the first time in months that I'm actually coming home without a stomach ache, a headache, and who-knows-what-all that aches. It's the first time in a long time that I'm coming home cancer-free.

It's a good feeling.

We step out of the car, and Mackenzie clutches my hand as we climb the great white steps onto the porch. The floor of the balcony above looms gray-white over us.

Dad opens the front door and we step inside. No one says a word.

The last time I came home, Dad carried me through this door and straight up to bed. This time, my eyes aren't blurry and my head isn't swimming. I look around.

Straight ahead, the lounge opens up in front of me. Sunshine streams through the rows of huge windows.

An archway to the left separates the dining room, with its rich oak paneling and sturdy furniture, from the lounge. Beyond that lies the great kitchen with its copper stove and granite counters and delicious smells.

Such smells are currently wafting in from that direction, and I know Mamie must be cooking up a feast for supper.

Riley laughs at Mackenzie and me. "Come on, you two look like you've forgotten what this house looks like!" he says.

I poke him. "Well, I almost have," I say, but he's broken the spell that made us stand so still and silent in our own home.

Mackenzie races me up the staircase beyond the lounge. I'm eager to see if our room looks the same as I remember it. Not the way it looked through pain filled eyes and long, sleepless nights, but the way it looked before.

I throw open the door. Two twin beds sit side-by-side beneath white canopies. The blue-cushioned window seat is still there.

Mackenzie runs eagerly to the window.

"Look, Taylor!" she squeals.

Down below, I can see the creek threading its way through the lush spring grass. In the nearest pasture, two bay horses are trotting along the fence. They toss their dainty heads and pick up their feet; their manes swirl in the breeze.

"Oakley and Stormy!" I yell. Mackenzie dances a little jig around the room.

"I can't wait to ride Oakley again," she gasps finally, falling across her bed.

I stare out at our horses again. I just hope Stormy remembers me.

Riley sticks his head in the doorway just then. "Dinner is ready," he says, flashing us his lightning grin.

We race downstairs.

The dining room is covered with a white lace cloth and set with the good china. It looks fit for a king...or two queens.

Mamie comes in, carrying a platter heaped high with fried chicken. Her large, brown eyes twinkle as she sets it before me.

"I'll get some fat on those bones of yours, yet," she grins.

I grin back. Mackenzie and I lost so much weight during our battle with cancer. We weighed ourselves at the hospital before we came home and we were both exactly seventy-seven pounds. Before cancer, I was over ninety.

Because it's such a special day, Mom insists that the servants join us for supper. While some of the folks around here are still stuck in pre-Civil War days, our servants are treated more like family.

Mamie and her husband, Charlie, who helps tend the horses, sit at the foot of the table. Rachel, the housekeeper, sits on one side while Rebecca, the gardener, and Thomas, Charlie and Mamie's son, sit on the other side.

I join hands with Rebecca on my left, and with Mackenzie on the other side, and bow my head while Dad blesses the food. His prayer seems to go on forever, and I think he thanks God for health at least three times, but for once, I don't really care.

I'm starving, so I pile my plate high with fried chicken, potatoes, and corn. But my skinny little body can only handle about a third of it. The doctors told us this would happen, but I didn't realize I could only handle *this* little pile of food.

I glance worriedly at Mamie. I hope she isn't offended by how little I take. Nothing is wrong with her food, after all.

She just smiles at me.

"You just wait another month or so, and you'll be rivaling Thomas with your plateful, child," is all she says.

After supper, even though it is only seven o'clock, I stumble up to bed. I'm exhausted.

2

Chapter 2

The pale, early morning sunlight streams through the stable windows.

Riley heaves the saddle up on Stormy's back, while the horse stands quietly. "Are you sure this is a good idea?" Riley asks, looking sideways at me.

I nod. "I can at least sit on a horse's back. It'll be fine. We'll stay in the corral and you can lead me."

Riley wouldn't let me handle the horse on my own, anyways -that much I knew. It would tire me out too much and if something happened and Stormy acted up- well, I'm not strong enough yet to handle that sort of thing.

Mackenzie is still sound asleep, but I, always an early riser, couldn't wait to see my horse. Riley pulls the cinch tight and yanks the stirrup down. He snaps on the lead and hands it to me.

I rubbed Stormy's neck one last time. "Come on, girl, let's hit it," I whispered.

Outside in the corral, Riley helps me up on Stormy's back. I never realized before how much energy it takes to mount a horse, but I managed to get up there.

I stick my boots in the stirrups and grin at Riley. It feels so good to be on a horse again. Riley leads me around and around in the corral until I get tired out, which isn't very long. But it feels good to be riding again, with the breeze blowing through my hair and the early-morning sun.

I trudge to the house as he unsaddles Stormy.

I am almost at the side door when far above me a dark, tousled head pokes out of an upstairs window, and an indignant voice calls, "Taylor Brooke Everett, were you riding without me?"

I grin at her and give a saucy wave. "You bet, sleepyhead!" I called back.

When I get inside, Mamie has just finished setting a steaming platter of scrambled eggs on the kitchen table, and Mom is sitting down sleepily, still in her robe. All the servants have already eaten, and Dad is outside on the range, counting cattle.

The kitchen is warm and cozy, with Mamie bustling around between the oven and the table, making sure we stuff ourselves for the day.

We always eat breakfast and lunch in the kitchen, often with the servants. Mom only insists dinner be in the more formal dining room. I guess it's the one bit of colonial mistress-ness that stayed with her through the years.

After a delicious breakfast, Mackenzie hauls me up to our room. She yanks open the middle drawer of our dresser. Hats, headbands, bows and wigs of every color and design spill out. "We need to decide what to wear for our first day of school," she announces importantly.

Although we will have to repeat Grade Eight next year because we missed so much school, I'm still excited to be there to see the year finish. A few months ago I hadn't even known if I'd be alive at all, let alone going to school. It's a triumph of sorts.

Mackenzie pulls on a neon pink, orange, and green striped wig.

"How's this?" she asks, parading around the room.

I wrinkle my nose at her. "You're not wearing that to school, Mac," I said.

She laughs and tips her head. "Mackenzie Everett will be the first student at Edison Junior and Senior High to have striped hair," she says in her best newscaster voice.

I stick my tongue out at her and pull on an auburn ponytail.

"Well, *Taylor* will be the first Everett to be a redhead," I announce in a snooty voice.

That makes both of us crack up.

"Where's the wig you were wearing this morning when you yelled at me out the window?" I ask.

"Oh, that's the one made from my real hair," she answers. She points to the dresser.

Two mannequin heads sat there, with long, wavy locks falling in dark brown pools around them. "Maybe we should just wear those for our first day," I say with uncertainty.

Mackenzie raises one eyebrow at me. "And miss your chance to be the first Everett at Edison High with red hair? You're not chickening out on me, are you, Taylor?"

I shove down my insecure feelings and grin. "Not unless you are!"

○○ ○○ ○○ ○○ ○○

Edison Junior and Senior High looks about the same as when we left it only a month into the school term in October last year, except in May, flowers are blooming instead of the crisp fall leaves that surrounded the red brick building last time.

Red wig firmly in place, I clutch Mackenzie's hand as we step out of the SUV. Mom blows us a kiss before heading out onto the street.

"Tayyyylor! Mackennnzie!" a high voice calls out, and our friend Allie comes running towards us. Her hug almost bowls me over.

"How ya guys doing? Man, it's good to have you two back."

Mackenzie grins at her and swishes her braid over her shoulder. "How do you like my hair?" she asks.

"I love it!" Allie cries. "Especially the purple. I just didn't want to mention it, cause, you know..."

She shrugs awkwardly and lets her sentence trail off.

I laugh and grab her arm. "Don't worry about offending us," I say.

Allie leads us both through the big double doors and up to the second floor, where most of the Grade seven and eight classes are. Our homeroom teacher, Miss Jamison, is standing at the door to Room 204.

"Hello, girls. Good to see y'all," she beams.

"Hi, Miss Jamison," Mackenzie grins. "I missed you- all except for those Math assignments you used to give us."

Miss Jamison just laughs and pats Mackenzie's shoulder.

The classroom looks the same, yet different inside. My desk is still in the same place- middle of the third row- but the bulletin boards and art on the walls are all different. It feels like the first day of school, again.

The bell rings just then, and kids pile into the classroom. They all stop and say 'hi' to Mackenzie and I. I'm glad her desk is right across from mine, because all the attention is starting to get a little overwhelming, and I need her close by.

Mason, this really cute guy that I've liked since Grade Five, sits down in his seat in front of me, then immediately turns around and gives me a smile. At the front, Miss Jamison claps her hands for silence, but he ignores her.

"Everything's pretty much the same old, same old," he whispers. "The aristocrats are still annoying, Miss Jamison still gives too much homework, and I still suck at baseball."

"Mason Gregory!" Miss Jamison barks, rapping on her desk. "Are you trying to get Taylor detention on her first day back?"

"She didn't say anything," he protests.

"Well, kindly turn around and listen, Mason. Some days I can't tell the difference between you kids and the first graders I used to teach."

Mason turns around sheepishly. Across the aisle, Mackenzie wiggles her eyebrows at me and mouths, "I think he likes you." I can feel redness creeping up my neck as I give her a mock glare.

Miss Jamison hands out a worksheet for English, next. She puts one on my desk and tells me and Mackenzie to just do our best and see how much of the stuff is new or we can't remember.

When I was first diagnosed with leukemia, I tried keeping up with my homework, but as I got sicker, it got harder and harder until I finally just stopped altogether. It's been at least three months since I've cracked open a book, and it's amazing how fast you forget stuff.

I chew the eraser at the end of my pencil, searching for prepositions in sentences, when Mason spins around in his seat again. He glances over at the teacher, who is helping someone on the other side of the room, before whispering to me.

"I really like your wig," he whispers.

"Ya, I'm thinking I might just shave my head for the rest of my life and wear wigs. Then I can look however I want, depending on my mood."

He squints his eyes at me for a second; then, obviously deciding I'm just kidding, he grins.

"Did it hurt?" he asks then, a little tentative.

"It felt like a hippo put me in its mouth, chewed me up, then dumped me off a cliff onto concrete," I tell him, giving him a grin.

"That's not funny," he says. "It sounds awful."

I shrug. "It was what it was, but that part's over now." I don't mention the fact that it could come back anytime. He doesn't have to worry about that.

"Mason!" Miss Jamison says, sounding exasperated. "I know you've missed Taylor, but *please*, you can talk to her at recess.

Mason quickly turns around in his chair, his ears red. Across the aisle, Mackenzie gives me a smirk and flutters her eyelashes. I ignore her and turn back to my prepositions.

∞ ∞ ∞ ∞ ∞

When I get home from school, I head right up to bed. I'm exhausted. I wonder how long it will take to fully regain my strength. Or what if it never happens? What if, by the next appointment, I've relapsed, and I have to go through this all over again?

Then I remember the Bible verse Mom taped to our bathroom mirror a few years ago. It was something about how God watches even the sparrows, so He can easily take care of me.

I shrug the scary thoughts out of my head and fall asleep.

3

Chapter 3

"Taylor, run!" Mackenzie hisses.

I duck behind a bush as a dark shadow slides by.

Farther up the stone pathway, the lanterns illuminate the face of Allie, my best friend.

Tomorrow is the last day of school, and Allie is having Mackenzie and I, and Ellie and Remy over for the night. We were playing cops-and-robbers in the dark with Allie's two younger brothers, Micah and Dayton.

The lantern bounces its rays off Ellie's blonde head as she and Allie circle the backyard, searching for their "robbers".

I crouch behind a tree beside Mackenzie, trying to breath as quietly as I can. She winks at me and pulls a plastic shopping bag out from between the roots of the great oak tree. "I hid this before we started the game," she whispers as she opens the bag carefully.

Inside are two gray wigs and a gray beard.

"They're looking for two girls, not two old men," Mackenzie explains, grinning at me.

I choke back a laugh of my own and pull on a short gray wig. "Where did you get these?" I ask Mackenzie.

She just gives me a lopsided smile, her teeth flashing white in the darkness.

"I pulled them out of the costume trunk at home. You never know when these things might come in handy."

Suddenly, I have an idea.

"Let's sneak over to those fields, and…" I whisper my plan to Mackenzie.

Her eyes light up.

"Let's go! You lead the way, Taylor." We dash through the trees, along the fence line, and over to a creek that runs through the field.

I dig up some mud from the bank and smear it over Mackenzie. Soon she blends into the night. Only the whites of her eyes gleam in the pale moonlight.

By the time I was brown, too, we could hear Allie and Ellie yelling in the distance. "Come on, guys, where are you?" Their voices echo off a nearby building.

I give Mackenzie a mischievous grin and grab a big stick.

∞ ∞ ∞ ∞ ∞

Two shadowy blobs crept back along the fence. The one with the beard seemed to favor its right leg while the other one leaned heavily on a stick.

The two figures came down the stone path.

Allie and Ellie came running at the sound of footsteps and the tapping of the stick on the stone.

The two girls shrieked as the figures came into the circle of lamplight. Two brown, stooped men with eerily shining eyes stared back at them.

The bearded one raised a hand. "We mean you no harm," the figure said in a quavering voice.

"We only want to know if you have any spare gasoline around," the old person with the stick added.

The two girls stepped back a little.

Mackenzie gives me a sideways glance, and her mouth curves a little under the gray beard. We were really scaring them.

I wave my stick in the air. "We only want a little gasoline and maybe some gunpowder," I say. Beside me, Mackenzie almost chokes.

"We will work for it. We simply need materials to make our bombs," I say calmly, as though it is the most everyday thing to request bomb making materials.

Allie's eyes are huge by now, and Ellie looked like she could cry.

Mackenzie winks at me and takes a step forward. "Now, now, honey," she quavers, "we don't mean no harm. Surely two sweets like you could...
"

Just then something rockets out of the shadows and slams me to the ground. The impact knocks the breath out of me.

Before I can react, the person is straddling me. I looked up into the grim face of Allie's little brother Micah.

"What do you want?" he demands. Beside me Mackenzie is in a similar position, with Dayton straddling her. I try to lift my arm up, but Micah holds on.

"Get off, Micah," I say in my normal voice. "Is this how you treat all of your sister's friends?"

He gets a shocked look on his face as he rolls off.

Mackenzie and I laugh as we get up. Allie looks surprised, and Ellie looks mad, but they can't help but join in.

"You should have seen your faces," Mackenzie gasps, doubling over with laughter.

Just then Remy appears from the trees. "How did you two get so muddy?" she asks, confused. Everyone else bursts into laughter.

I guess my sister and I were born with a little bit of a mischievous streak.

◯◯ ◯◯ ◯◯ ◯◯ ◯◯

The sun shines overhead as we head back to the bayou bordering Allie's farm. Beside us, the short, grassy looking sugarcane plants sway in the breeze. Mackenzie and I are riding in the back of the pickup with Remy, while Allie drives and Ellie keeps her company in the cab.

We bounce over a rut, and Remy yelps as her shin hits the hump over the wheel.

"They should put cushions in these things," she jokes.

Mackenzie yawns. "What time did we actually fall asleep then last night?" she wonders.

"I saw two am on the clock before I conked out," I shrug, "But I don't know when anyone else fell asleep."

Remy nods. "I love sleepovers, except that you always feel horrible by the next evening."

The truck bounces into the grove of bald cypress surrounding the waters of Bayou Lafourche, and instantly the air gets cooler. We pull up beside a rack of kayaks near the water, and get out.

Allie pulls an old, fading red kayak off the rack and shoves it over to Ellie.

"That one's a double seater. Remy, do you want to share it with Ellie? She's never kayaked before."

"Unless you count sitting on my Dad's lap while he paddled around a tiny lake at our cottage back when I was three," Ellie laughs.

Mackenzie and I have taken several boating trips down the bayou with our family over the years, so we each grab a single kayak and shove it down to the water after Allie. Ellie and Remy are struggling to get their kayak into the water amidst the cypress trunks.

"Come over here," Mackenzie calls to her. "There's a nice little shore here to launch off of."

I drag my boat over to her, getting it caught in a pile of exposed tree

16

roots in the process. Mackenzie and Allie are standing on a little gravel bar that sticks out into the brackish waters of the slow moving bayou.

"There used to be a bridge across here," Allie explains as we get into our kayaks. "It went all the way over to the other shore. It wasn't very strong, though, and in a rainstorm it all got washed away. That little gravel bar and a random post in the middle of the bayou are all that's left of it."

I dip a paddle into the dark waters of the bayou and push off for the middle of the swamp. It's peaceful and quiet out here. The bayou waters don't have enough of a current to make a sound, and the trees around us make me feel like I'm sailing down a hallway with cypress walls.

A fish jumps off to the left, and frogs croak from somewhere in the bayou. A warm, gentle spring breeze tickles my face.

"So...how are you guys liking going to school again?" Ellie asks me and Mackenzie.

"It's been great!" Mackenzie says enthusiastically.

"Even though we only get to be there for the last two weeks, it feels good to see our classmates again before summer," I add.

"I really like how you wear different hair every day to school," Remy giggles. "I don't know if I would be able to embrace being bald like that."

I shrug. "We can't change the fact that we don't have much hair right now, so we decided we may as well have fun with it."

"It's just good to be out of the hospital again," Mackenzie says.

We all fall silent again, entranced by the magic of the bayou. It's like a whole different world out here.

"Look! Over by that huge cypress trunk!" Allie suddenly whispers loudly. "An alligator!"

I scan the area she's pointing to, and sure enough– two beady eyes are looking at us from just above the waterline. The rest of the alligator's body is buried under the water, except for a bit of bumpy back that looks very much like a log protruding from the bayou.

We paddle carefully and quietly around the alligator. It's mating season right now, and the gators can be especially aggressive this time of year. The beady eyes don't leave us until we round a bend out of sight.

We paddle on for a while, and as we get closer to town, we meet more and more kayakers. The trees start to thin out, and we can now see the cars roaring by us on St. Mary's Street.

"Should we turn around?" Allie asks as we pass under the Lafourche Crossing, an old train bridge spanning the bayou.

"It's a long way back," Mackenzie agrees, "And I'm starting to get hungry."

Allie leads the way back down the river, and we enter the peaceful water 'hallway' between the trees once again.

"Look! Another alligator!" Ellie cries out excitedly.

"Shhh!" Allie hisses. "You'll scare it."

Ellie, who's in the front of her and Remy's kayak, cranes her neck towards the alligator.

"It's a little one!" she says, this time a little more quietly.

"Ellie, watch where you're-" I try to warn my friend, but it's too late. Their kayak rams into a cypress trunk and capsizes. The alligator sinks beneath the surface of the water and disappears.

Ellie and Remy splash around the water after their kayak as it drifts away. The bayou isn't very deep in this part, thankfully, but the bottom is mucky, and Remy loses a flip-flop in the mud as she grabs the kayak.

"Oh man, I am so sorry," Ellie says to Remy as they both scramble up the slippery bank with their kayak in tow.

"Whatever," Remy says shortly. "Can't do anything about it now."

I paddle over with Allie to help hold their kayak against the bank as they get back in. Remy doesn't look too happy to be sopping wet, and Ellie looks like she could cry. They don't speak to each other for the rest of the way back.

Back at Allie's house, we eat a silent lunch and then Mackenzie and I go upstairs to pack our bags up. Mom is picking us up right after lunch for a dentist appointment, and for once I'm glad to be leaving a sleepover early. The mood downstairs isn't exactly sunny between Remy and Ellie, and Allie just kind of sits there awkwardly because she doesn't know what to do.

"Hopefully they get it figured out down there," Mackenzie whispers in my ear as we head down the stairs.

"Yah," I agree.

We lug our stuff downstairs, say goodbye to our friends, and head out the door to the waiting car.

"How was the sleepover?" Mom asks brightly.

"Don't ask," I groan.

∞ ∞ ∞ ∞ ∞

It's the last day of school. Mackenzie and I decide to go all out in the wig department, so when we pull out our crazy, neon, stripey wigs, our friends just about lose it. (Ellie and Remy have made up with each other—thankfully).

Allie's dad drives us to school in the nearby town of Thibodaux. When Mackenzie and I walk into class, we get a standing ovation for our hair. Then Miss Jamison gets up to deliver her usual end of the year speech before we party.

"I know it hasn't been a good year for everybody, but we trust that next year will be even better," she begins. I glance at Mackenzie out of the corner of my eye. *I* hope that next year will be better, too, but the problem is that it easily might not be.

We're in remission, but we aren't cured. There is always the risk of relapsing, and it has become my biggest fear. I zone in again as Miss Jamison finishes her speech.

"To end our year of school, I want everyone to say one thing they are looking forward to doing this summer," she says.

One by one, we go around the room. A lot of kids say swimming or boating down the bayou. A few of the rich types, like Evangeline Turner or Arrabelle Richards, say balls or garden parties. Mackenzie says she can't wait to go stargazing on our roof in the summer. I say I'm looking forward to lots of horseback riding.

Then a couple of kids help her bring out the snacks, and the real fun begins. We consume way too much sugar, laugh like middle-schoolers, and try to catch popcorn in our mouths. Mason even compliments my hair, and he's serious, not mocking. He says he thinks it's great, and he might have to get himself a matching wig.

As I walk to my locker at the end of the day with a backpack full of books, I feel a tap on my shoulder. It's Marissa Lambert, the student president and valedictorian graduate.

"Hi, Taylor, it's so good to see you back in school!" she says with a voice as sweet as honey. "We're so happy you were able to finish out the year here."

I nod warily, but inside I am wondering why Marissa cares.

She pats my shoulder. "Have a great summer," she says, and then she is gone.

I shake my head. I sure don't know what that was all about. Four teachers do the same thing to Mackenzie and I as we walk out of school. I hate it. We're cancer survivors; we aren't zoo animals. I know they're just trying to be nice, but it makes me feel awkward.

I guess everyone feels like they should congratulate us for being alive, or something.

II

June

June is the gateway to summer.
-Jean Hersey

4

Chapter 4

Last June, I was sitting in the emergency room with what I thought was a bad flu. Last June, I was undergoing a battery of tests. Last June, I found out I have leukemia.

This June everything feels bigger and brighter. I actually feel the summer breeze as it ripples through the grass and whistles over the great oaks and lob lolly pines. I notice the Queen Anne's Lace, nodding her white head while butterflies dance around in the sunshine. I can smell the sweetness of wildflowers in the wind.

The promise of summer makes me feel giddy, like a kid on a sugar high. When I hop out of bed on the first day of June, the one thing I feel like doing is jumping on my horse and riding back to the forest with the wind in my hair. Mackenzie and I hurriedly braid each other's hair-sorry, wigs,-and creep down the stairs and out the back hall. If Mom or Mamie saw us, they'd sit us on a kitchen chair and make us eat a hearty breakfast. I am a little hungry, but not enough to take up riding time.

We run to the stable and duck around the corner, breathing hard.

"Don't let Dad see us," Mackenzie whispers.

A door slams shut at the other end of the barn, and I release a breath I didn't know I was holding.

"I think that was Dad going in for breakfast!" I hiss back.

We saddle our horses in record time. Heaving a saddle up onto Stormy's back reminds me that I'm not as hardy as I used to be, but there's no time like the present for regaining strength.

It's our first ride together, alone, since last spring when cancer hit. The horses seem to sense our excitement, and they prance eagerly. Stormy tosses her head as if to say, "Come on, I'm ready to run."

We lead the horses out behind the stables-still out of sight of the house- and mount our steeds.

"Race you to the forest!" I call over my shoulder as I loosen the reins and tap my heels on Stormy's sides. She takes off, the wind rushing past my face.

There's nothing quite like racing through the grass under the blue sky on horseback. Lines of wooden fence posts march along in a line, like an army on parade. Wild daisies and buttercups sway in the breeze. Oakley and Stormy are neck and neck, straining for the lead.

The path turns to dirt, and tall southern oaks begin to stand up on either side. The horses slow to a steady trot. The staccato of hoof beats reminds of my heart, beating steadily in my now healthy body.

The trees grow denser and the air cooler, as we enter the forest. We slow the horses even more, down to a walk. Shadows dance and sunlight sifts down through the green foliage.

Tall trees press in on either side of the trail. Their branches stretch toward each other in friendly greeting, almost like old pals sticking up for each other. Purple clover and wild cone flowers dot the forest floor. Off to the left, I can hear the rushing of the river as it spills over the rocks and crevices of the creek bed.

"Hey, look!" Mackenzie yells, pointing off to the right.

A faint trail disappears off into the woods. It's choked with weeds and grasses, and nearly invisible. I've ridden in this forest many times over the years, but never seen it before.

"Let's follow it!" I call back, pushing Stormy forward. Her hooves trod carefully along the almost invisible trail. Mackenzie and Oakley ride along behind me.

I feel like Columbus, exploring a new land, or maybe like a caravan leader, guiding our load of exotic spices along a treacherous route. The trees are now impossibly close together, and the bush is dark.

The twisting trail leads us to a small clearing. The grass in it is shaggy and long, the stems just starting to show bubbles where the seed heads will be. I dismount and loop Stormy's reins over a stump. She gratefully bends her head and begins grazing.

"This place is creepy," Mackenzie whispers, coming up beside me. "I never knew our farm held something like this."

The clearing is shadowy and dark. "Yeah," I whisper back. I point silently to a dead lob lolly pine on the other side of the clearing. "Reminds me of a scarecrow," I whisper.

My twin sister slides a cold hand into mine. "Should we go back?" she asks.

I shake my head. My curiosity is growing by the minute.

"Come on, Mac. Let's explore this place first. We're the first ones here in a long time."

"No kidding."

We walk slowly through the clearing. In the fall, I'm guessing it will be covered in burr bushes and stickers, but in spring, it's pretty easy walking. Near the center, we find a small stone platform of sorts. Just beyond that I suddenly stop.

"Look," I whisper, pointing. A pair of rusty metal shackles are lying on the ground. Out of the corner of my eye I see something glinting in the sunlight. I reached over and picked it up. A dull gold chain hangs from my fingers, a key dangling from it.

"What is this?" Mackenzie whispers.

"I don't know," I say. "Let's get out of here." We walk quickly over to our horses. My sense of curiosity is totally gone, now, replaced by a sense of foreboding.

Suddenly Mackenzie goes sprawling on the grass.

"Mac! Are you okay?" I ask anxiously, leaning down to give her a hand up.

Mackenzie nods. "I just tripped on something. Look!"

She points to the ground near her feet. The metal corner of a box is protruding out of the dirt.

"Let's dig it up and see what it is!" I whisper as I drop to my knees. Mackenzie and I dig furiously in the dirt for a few minutes until we uncover the object.

A small oblong box, made entirely out of metal, soon rests in Mackenzie's lap. A tiny lock holds its clasps together securely. It's encrusted with dirt, and rusty. It looks very old.

"Do you think it's a time capsule from the 1800s?" Mackenzie guesses.

I shrug skeptically. "I don't know if that was a thing back then. How about I get a rock and try to break the lock open," I suggest.

"No, wait, Taylor. Try the key we found."

The lock is a little dirty, and the key is a bit rusty, but they are both in surprisingly good shape, considering they've been in the dirt for who-knows-how-long. But with a bit of jiggling around, we're able to get it open.

I lift the box's cover. Inside lies a mishmash of old, yellow papers.

∞ ∞ ∞ ∞ ∞

1849 June 9
Dear Diary,
Today Kitty got sent to the fields. Massa Andrews found she could read

some, and he don't like that.

Kitty is my biggest sister, and she's my role model of sorts. She's the one who helps me and touches up for me if I miss something in the Big House.

Massa Andrews is okay for a massa, least I know there's worse, but them white folks don't like a slave to be able to read and write. Gives us too much power, I guess. They's scared of losing control of us.

I can't ever let Massa or Missy Andrews catch on that I can read, or that Mama and Kitty taught me, neither. We'd both be sent off to who knows where in the blink of an eye. Or whipped to death on the spot.

Old George says Louisiana is a fine enough place for a slave. Round here, least they ain't allowed to separate families, according to written law at least. Not that written law stops most folks, but it's a start.

Old George has been all over. He says Alabama was his worst nightmare, and we're lucky here. Old George has enough scars on his back to make his words believable. He can spin a yarn that'll send shivers down your spine, and he claims they's all true stories.

I found this empty exercise schoolbook in the trash when I took it out from Priscilla's room (she's Massa's daughter) so I'm gonna write in it near often as possible, and hide it away in this old hollow hickory. Maybe someday, if'n I get free, I can come back and read of these days. I think maybe, someday, if'n us slaves ever get free in this country, these words will be valuable.

Prissy is calling for me, so I reckon I'd better go.

Nora Mae Washington

5

Chapter 5

It's one thing to learn about the lives of slaves in history class; it's quite another to hold the diary of a slave girl in your hands.

The binding of the book is old; the pages fragile. Mackenzie and I turn them carefully. "Wow," Mackenzie whispered. "We're holding a piece of history."

I carefully place the papers back into the box. I hang the key around my neck, while Mackenzie snaps the lock back on.

"Let's take it to our room and just read it bit by bit," she suggests.

"Good idea! When we're done, if the diary isn't too sad, we can show it to Charlie and Mamie. Their grandparents were slaves, so maybe they want to read it, too," I say.

Mackenzie sticks the box carefully into her saddlebag. "Until then, let's hide it," she says. "We don't want Mom or Dad giving it away to Charlie and Mamie if everybody dies in it."

I nod as I climb into the saddle. As we ride out of the dark clearing, I think about how sad parts of our history are. *My home* might have been a slave plantation once. Thankfully, the woods become friendlier the further away from the clearing we get. It feels good to leave the darkness behind.

When we get back to the stable, I start unsaddling Stormy while my sister wraps the box up in her sweater and runs to the house. Riley follows Mackenzie back and helps us unsaddle. "You got an invitation to a party," he tells us.

"Oh?" I say curiously, glad there is no mention of us not being present at the breakfast table. Riley would have warned us if Mom was too worried, or hopping mad.

He grins. "Yup... to the one and only Evangeline Turner."

I groan.

The Turners live on a large sugarcane plantation on the other side of Thibodaux. Their mother is still stuck in colonial days, and often hosts lavish parties and grand balls, complete with fancy gowns and those paper fan things that used to be all the rage.

Mrs. Turner takes pride in reminding everyone of the long line of wealthy and notable patriarchs of the Turner and Williams (her maiden name) families.

Her daughter, Evangeline, is the apple of her eye, and just as snooty. Unlike most of her other rich friends, she doesn't attend a private school, so Mackenzie and I have to endure her at school, too, although she usually just ignores our presence. But somehow Mom and Mrs. Turner happen to be friends. We aren't as rich as the Turner's, but despite how much influence your dollar value has on your place in the Turner circles, we somehow often get included in their parties. I guess Everett blood is aristocratic enough for them, or something.

I can't even begin to count the number of times Mackenzie and I have had to endure dainty tea parties in silk, flounced dresses at Evangeline's house, eating tiny cookies that don't fill you up and listening to her brag about her 'etiquette'. But, since Mr. Turner buys horses, and he and

Dad are business partners of sorts, we need to stay in good relations.

And besides, despite Mrs. Turner's bragging, my mom actually enjoys her parties. She's a bit of an aristocrat herself, and doesn't understand why Mackenzie and I hate getting dressed up in gowns to have tea. So we grin and bear it... and try to have a little fun along the way.

"It's Evangeline's birthday," Riley explains, "and of course she wants her *favourite* pair of twins to attend," he says dramatically, clasping his hands and rolling his eyes skyward.

"Why do we get *invited* to these things?" Mackenzie sighs. "Every party, we do something wrong, anyway."

At Evangeline's last party, our dresses were the wrong colour. They didn't match her 'vibes', or something like that. The time before, our shoes were 'out of style'. It's a wonder she still invites us to her house.

Riley reaches deep into his pocket and pulls out a slightly rumpled, dusty rose paper, and hands it to us.

"You are cordially invited to attend a celebration for Evangeline Turner on the Ninth of June, at the Turner household," I read.

"Who wrote that?" Mackenzie wonders. "Also, who actually talks like that anymore?"

"The Turners," Riley and I chorus.

Mackenzie sighs again.

◌◌ ◌◌ ◌◌ ◌◌ ◌◌

1849, June 16

Dear Dairy,

Prissy Andrews is such a worm! Now, I know you shouldn't call anyone a worm, but that's really what she is!

Asks me three times to make her bed "just so," then complains because it takes too long.

Then I do her hair up in a complicated French knot, only for her to make me take it down and do something else because she 'changed her mind'! But she didn't like that, so we ended up with the knot in the end, anyway.

When she finally came downstairs, Massa Andrews was mad because she was late for brunch. Plus, Lola- she's the cook- got a smidgen too much spice on his eggs, so that didn't help his mood none, either. Of course Prissy blamed her bein' late on me, and Massa Andrews threatened to send me to the fields.

I was in the fields for two years before I came to the Big House, and it was horrible. It's hard work cutting sugarcane or weeding the cotton, and if you slow at all, you get whipped. It's hot out there, and your throat gets so dry you feel like you'd give just 'bout anything for a cup of water.

Thankfully, Massa didn't go through with his threat. But after brunch Prissy wanted me to be her dog, and go for a walk in the courtyard, and I almost wished I was in the fields.

There is nothing more degrading than having to act like another person's animal. But I did it anyway, because I don't actually want to be sent to the fields.

Is fear and degradation all that's in life for a black person like me?
Nora Mae Washington

∞ ∞ ∞ ∞ ∞

I put the diary back in its box at the back of our closet and sigh. This Prissy girl sounds a lot like Evangeline Turner to me.

Mackenzie groans from the middle of the large closet.

"What do I wear?" she wails.

"Whatever you want," I retort. She gives me a look.

"Well, what are you wearing? she asks me.

I shrug and walk over to her. I grab the first thing my hand lands on in the sea of rarely-used silks and pull out a dark blue dress with a ruffled skirt and lots of ribbons.

"This," I answer.

Mackenzie laughs and shuts her eyes. She sticks a hand into the pile and pulls out a light green, flowery dress with ribbons and sparkles.

"Now for the wigs," she sighs. "Why is getting ready so *hard?*

"Cause you make it hard," I snap back. I'm already feeling unhappy about having to go to the party. I can't deal with a dramatic sister, too.

"Well, I'm just going to wear a headband," I reply. "Can you imagine Mrs. Turner's face when her dream of a beautiful ball birthday is shattered by a bald head? Smooth and shiny doesn't go so well with a fancy gown when it's your own bald head, but she can't say anything without sounding rude."

Mackenzie flashes me a smile of pure delight and begins rummaging through the headbands for a green one. She slips it on, and we run downstairs to say 'goodbye' to Mamie.

Mamie is in the kitchen, rolling out cinnamon bun dough. Her hands are covered with flour, and she has a dusting of cinnamon on one cheek.

She steps away from the counter and gives us the once-over.

"Love the dresses,girls, even though I know you prefer less fancy clothes."

Her eyes twinkle, as she says,"and I love what you two have done with your hair."

I look at my sister and we share a grin. I'm pretty sure Mamie is following our line of thinking. The Turners could use a little something different, anyway-break their stereotype of what a 'perfect party' requires.

We go into the lounge as Mom comes downstairs. She stares at us for a moment.

"You girls don't want.... hair?" she asked uncertainly.

Mackenzie puts on her best sad face.

"Mom, we don't have hair. Why pretend?" she asks in her best 'hurt' voice.

Mom smiles quickly. "Oh no, it's perfectly fine. I just thought maybe..." her voice trails off.

I bite back a smirk. This is working perfectly.

Thomas drives up with the Camaro just then. He's our unofficial chauffeur to these kinds of things. We don't go away enough to big parties to need a full-time chauffeur, and Dad or Mom are perfectly capable of driving to church or the grocery store, but for a Turner party, it seems to be a necessity. Mackenzie and I squeeze in the back while Mom sits primly in front.

It's a twenty minute drive to the Turner plantation. The closer we get, the hotter and more itchy my gown feels. I can't wait for this party to be over.

Mackenzie holds our gift on her lap. We're giving Evangeline this silk shawl thing that Mom found at *Pilot and Powell* during one of our New Orleans stays. It's some elegant, flimsy looking thing that cost almost three hundred dollars. I personally wouldn't wear it for ten thousand.

All too soon, Thomas is turning down a tree-lined lane. It leads to a huge colonial-style mansion, even bigger than our house. A few late model cars are already in the driveway when we pull in.

The Turner's butler greets us on the porch and tells Thomas he is welcome to join the other chauffeurs in the den to the right.

He directs us ladies to the north salon. Obviously some of Evangeline's private school friends are here. No one else would have a real chauffeur. I just hope they aren't all like Evangeline.

Mrs. Turner meets us at the door of the large north salon. She is dressed in a resplendent gold gown that shimmers in the light. Thousands of dollars worth of diamonds glitter from her wrists and ears. Someone is party *ready*.

Behind her, the salon is decorated in silver and pink, with streamers and balloons everywhere. Mrs. Turner clasps her hands together and gives us a little curtsy of sorts.

"Oh, it's so good to see you, Carolina," she says, greeting our mother.

Her smile flickers for only a moment as she turns to us.

"Oh, and the twins too. Evangeline will be so glad to see you," she says, recovering her bright smile. Her eyes keep straying to our bare heads, though. Finally, she just pats our shoulders.

"And we're all so glad you are healthy again!" she adds awkwardly as she pushes us into the room. I cringe inside and hope not everyone will feel the need to mention our cancer.

Evangeline comes rushing over in a pale pink gown, a jeweled crown on her head.

She hugs us and squeals, "Oh, I'm so glad you two are ba-a-ack!"

I feel a little embarrassed, especially as lavender and silver and midnight blue gowns turned our way.

For a second I almost wish we had decided to wear hair, but I tell myself we aren't and don't want to be a part of this crowd anyway, so what does it matter if they all laugh? For once, Evangeline actually seems genuinely glad to see us.

She leads us into the salon. In one corner, a big birthday banner hangs over a pink table full of presents. Mackenzie quickly puts ours beside the others.

We're the last guests to arrive, and Mrs. Turner quickly organizes us into a game of charades. Charades is an acting game which was popular in the Victorian Era, and since Mrs. Turner is stuck in those times, it's her favourite game.

We all sit down in a circle on the ballroom floor, trying to keep our gowns from getting too squashed. Evangeline somehow manages to be the starting actress, and proceeds to act like a half-deranged chipmunk on Red Bull (not that she would know what Red Bull is).

"See? I'm gliiiding," she announces as she does an awkward swoop to one side.

"You can't talk, Evangeline," a girl from the opposing team giggles.

"Are you....a figure skater?" someone guesses. I'm not sure where they got *that* out of Evangeline's performance.

"Noooo," Evangeline sighs dramatically. "Isn't it *obvious*?"

She does a few twirls, the skirt of her gown swirling out in a big circle.

"One of those spinning doll things in a music box," Mackenzie says sarcastically.

Evangeline whirls around.

"Yes, yes! Somebody said it! I'm a music box princess!"

On the chairs behind us, Mrs. Turner claps her hands together and squeals.

"Good job, darling! You looked *just* like a music box princess!"

I sure couldn't see the resemblance, but maybe I'm just blind. Since Mackenzie guessed the right thing, she gets to go next. She pulls a card out of the box and reads it, then makes a face at me. This could be good.

She proceeds to get down on all fours-I doubt any of the Turner children have ever done *that* before-and starts making the biggest racket ever. She growls and barks and moos, all while kicking her heels up and charging around the circle. I sneak at glance at Mrs. Turner. She's gone pale. I don't think Mom is too happy, either.

"A drunk!" Evangeline calls out.

"Evangeline!" her mother gasps in horror. "We don't talk about such things!"

By now, Mackenzie is red in the face from exertion, but she keeps on making weird noises and hopping around with the nimbleness of a gymnast. Her headband falls off and gets caught in her shoe. She tumbles onto her back, gasping for breath.

The room is dead silent for a moment, save for a few snickering noises from me and this other red-haired girl across the circle. A few girls' mouths are hanging open.

"Oookay," Evangeline finally breaks the silence. "What was *that*?"

"Certainly not a music box princess," another girl sniffs.

Mackenzie starts laughing.

"Well...the paper said a...Holstein dog...so I didn't know whether to be...a dog or a cow...so I was both."

That sets me and the redhead off again, and soon everyone is howling with laughter, except, of course, Evangeline and her mother. I even see Mom biting back a smile.

We laugh until tears stream down our cheeks, and our sides hurt. And Evangeline wades into the middle of it all, trying to gain back the attention at *her* party.

"It was just a mistake! It's not *funny*!" she yells. "This isn't funny! Stop laughing, everyone!"

Finally, she just sits down and sulks until the laughter dies down.

The charades game is over for the day after that, and Mrs. Turner quickly turns us towards the presents, obviously hoping to put the spotlight back on her daughter. We all sit on plush cushions in a semi-circle around Evangeline while she tears into her gifts.

"Oooh! A premium leather-grain journal and a fountain pen!...Oh, I've been wanting these shoes for a long time!...Mom, look at this! It's the shawl I've been begging you for! Did you see, Mom? Mom?"

The expensive presents seem to bring back Evangeline's good mood, and she even thanks Mackenzie and I for the 'absolutely *stunning* wrap.'

After the presents, we all troop over to the dining room for 'tea', as Mrs. Turner calls it- essentially a fancy word for a snack.

The table is covered with a pale pink cloth, and set with fine china and silver. A gray balloon is tied to the chair at the head of the table, for the birthday girl. The table seems to groan under the mounds of food on it- cut-glass pitchers of punch and lemonade, macarons, cookies of every variety, spiced cakes and breads and jams, and, at the center of the table, a three-tier chocolate cake, all exquisitely decorated.

"That looks yummy," I mutter in Mackenzie's ear. "I can't wait to dive into that cake."

Mrs. Turner seats us all at the table, with the adults at the end.

"Before we begin, let us ask a blessing on the food and the birthday girl." Mrs. Turner bows her head, and we all follow suit. After a lengthy blessing for Evangeline, with a thankyou-for-the-food thrown in at the end, we all dive in.

Midway through the snack, a strange scuffling comes from down the hall. I glance around the table, but no one else seems to have noticed, so I turn back to my cake.

Suddenly, a little ball of brown and black hurtles into the dining room, jumps up on my lap, and scarfs down my chocolate cake. The little dog then looks up at me with a satisfied smile, licking the icing off her lips. I stare back, a little stunned.

"Princess!"Evangeline shrieks, darting from her chair. The little Yorkie just cocks her head.

"What is that *dog* doing at the table?" Mrs. Turner exclaims sharply.

Evangeline plucks the dog out of my lap and snuggles her in her arms.

"Oh, Princess, did you escape from the study? You're a naughty little-Mom! She ate the chocolate cake! She's gonna dieeeee!!"Evangeline ends her speech with a sob.

Mrs. Turner goes pale for the second time that day, as she rises from her chair.

"Uh...my apologies, guests, but it looks like we have a little emergency here. I'm afraid we'll have to cut this party short."

I try to apologize to Evangeline. I feel a little responsible, since the dog ate my piece of cake, but Evangeline is too busy sobbing into Princess' fur to answer.

Mom grabs me by the elbow and steers Mackenzie and I toward the door.

"Thanks for having us, Mrs. Turner," she calls over her shoulder.

"Uh...you're welcome. Don't worry about the dog, Taylor. It isn't your fault. Oh, and the chauffeurs are in that room down the hall."

Mrs. Turner's voice fades as we head for the door. We manage to locate Thomas to drive us home, and thankfully let ourselves out. Mackenzie and I climb in the back of the car and I lean my head back and grin shakily at my twin sister.

"Well...how's that for a little excitement?"

6

Chapter 6

1849, June 21

Dear Diary,

Prissy had a big party yesterday for her birthday, and it was horrible. All her little friends came in their fancy gowns, and they giggled something fierce and talked 'bout nothing. And instead of one Prissy bossing me around, I had ten!

Of course, Prissy had to make a show of me because I'm 'her' slave. So she got me up in front of all her friends and asked if I've ever tasted a birthday cake before. 'Course I said I hadn't, and I think she knew that, so she cut out a big piece. First I thought she was finally being nice, cause it was her birthday and all, but I should have known something was up. Prissy is never nice.

She got me a fork and I took a big bite. And wow, it tasted good! It was very sweet, but I like sweet things. And the cake was so fluffy and light; it was like eating a cloud. Then she asks if it was good, and I say it was amazing. Then she grabs the plate from my hands and her face gets all mean, and she says pigs like me don't deserve cake. Then she went out and fed it to her dog, like the dog deserved cake, but not me.

My daddy always says you gotta forgive, even when it's hard, cause that's what Jesus did. But I think I'm gonna need a lot of help forgiving Prissy Andrews.

But I do think that someday, if I ever make it to freedom, the first thing I wanna eat is a big piece of birthday cake.

Nora Mae Washington

○○ ○○ ○○ ○○ ○○

Grandpa and Grandma Charlton, my mom's parents, are coming up for the weekend to see us now that we're out of the hospital. They wanted to come earlier, but Mom was able to push it off until now. She used all kinds of excuses, but at the end of the day, they're still our grandparents, and they deserve to see us every once in a while.

Grandpa and Grandma Charlton live in a huge mansion in Georgia. And maybe it's a little disrespectful to say this about my own grandparents, but they're horrible.

Grandma Charlton is a very opinionated woman who is every bit an aristocrat, and tends to look down on everyone else who isn't fortunate enough to have been born with 'good blood'. She's the kind who believes that having servants is her 'right' and wouldn't pay them if she didn't have to. She's a real snob.

Grandpa Charlton is better, but his wife has made him just a shadow of a man. He comes from a long line of decorated war veterans, right back to the Civil War, and rarely speaks. He's a strong, thoughtful man underneath, though, I think; his wife just never lets him get any of that out. Between him and Grandma, I'm not sure how they managed to raise a kid as nice and well-rounded as Mom.

At six this morning, Grandma called to let us know that they boarded the train in Atlanta for the thirteen hour trip to New Orleans, and could we please be at the station in New Orleans to pick them up around seven tonight? They were originally going to drive out, but Grandma changed her mind last week because the train is cheaper, and despite being rich, she is very stingy.

At breakfast, Mom tells us that she and Dad planned a day trip to New Orleans, and we'll leave right after breakfast. Mackenzie and Riley are super excited, but I'm not sure if I'm ready to go back to that particular city again so soon.

But the plans are already made, and we all get ready after breakfast while Dad fills the SUV up with gas.

"We should match today," Mackenzie suggests in our room. "I mean, we're going back to the city where we almost died, so we may as well celebrate that we're coming back alive."

I roll my eyes at her. "You are *so* weird," I tease. "Who wants to celebrate New Orleans? That place just reminds me of chemo and antiseptic."

Mackenzie laughs and throws me a plaid pink and black shirt that matches the one in her hand. "*You're* so weird," she shoots back. "Who *wouldn't* want to celebrate."

I pull on my black cowgirl boots and toss hers out of the back of the closet.

Mackenzie opens our wig drawer and rifles through it.

"Should we go black today? Or maybe Grandma Charlton would appreciate pink."

"How about white to match her?" I suggest, trying to keep a serious face on.

"We'd have to borrow one of *her* wigs to do that," Mackenzie answers. "But maybe this candy cane headband would be nice. Oh wait, we only have one. I guess maybe that's good, because we want to remind Grandma of her least favourite holiday."

"It would match *perfectly* with our plaid shirts," I add sarcastically.

"Girls! We're leaving in ten minutes!" Mom yells up the stairs.

We hastily pull on our wigs made from our real hair – the only ones

Mom would let us wear in front of Grandma Charlton anyway- and head downstairs.

"Oooohh, look at the twins!" Riley says in a high, sing-song voice. "Aren't they just *so* cute?!"

I punch him in the arm and tell him to go jump in the bayou. Dad comes in just then and herds us all out to the SUV. Mackenzie and I beat Riley outside and take the two middle seats. He grumbles at us but sits down in the back by himself.

"So where are we going in New Orleans?" Mackenzie asks Mom as we head out the lane. Mom just gives us this annoying little smile and says that it's a secret. I sigh loudly to let her know that I don't appreciate secrets. Riley just says we had better not be going to the zoo.

After a few arguments, we all settle down with our headphones on, and the next hour flies by. As we cross the Mississippi River, I take my headphones off and watch the passing scenery. It's a different part of town, but it still reminds me of going to the hospital. We had to cross the river, then, too.

I close my eyes and lean my head back against the headrest on my seat. Mom claps her hands, then, and I sit up. She motions for my siblings to take their headphones off, too.

"We're almost there, guys," she says. "Close your eyes."

"Ah, Mom, we're not little kids on a trip anymore. We don't need to close our eyes. The surprise can't be *that* big," Riley complains.

"Just shut your eyes," Mom insists.

"Help, Dad," Mackenzie groans. "Let us keep them open."

"Why, are you scared of the dark?" Dad teases. I roll my eyes at him through the rear view mirror. I quickly look out my window for any clues as to where we are in New Orleans before I shut my eyes, but all I can figure out is that we're somewhere in the French Quarter.

Dad takes a few turns before finally slowing to a crawl. He backs up into what I'm guessing is a parking spot.

"Can we open our eyes now?" Riley yells from the backseat.

"Uh-uh. Wait until we're out of the SUV," Dad says.

I feel around for my seat belt and unbuckle. Dad gets out and opens my door for me. Riley attempts to get out from the back with his eyes closed, and bangs his head on the roof.

"Ow!" He yells. "This is child abuse!" Dad just laughs and helps him out. Finally, they let us open our eyes.

In front of us is a huge, white building. A weird glass cylinder that looks like it had a slice cut out of it at an angle, rises up from one end. A big blue and white shark hovers over the entrance with the words *Audubon Aquarium of the Americas* beneath it.

"We're going to an aquarium? This is almost as bad as the zoo," Riley groans.

"This is cool!" is Mackenzie's opinion. "I've been wanting to see the underwater Mayan ruins exhibit ever since Allie told us about it two summers ago."

"This is way better than a zoo," I agree.

Mom grins. "Well, we aren't going just to see the fish. We're going to *swim* with the fish," she says.

"Really?!!" Mackenzie squeals.

"The aquarium has a program where you can snorkel in the Mayan Reef exhibit," Dad explains. "I happen to have a friend who works in the aquarium, and he was able to get us tickets on short notice."

"This is so cool!" I grab Mackenzie's hands and we do an impromptu jig around the SUV. Even Riley admits this might actually be fun, after all.

Mom pulls a big bag of towels and swimming suits from the trunk and hands it to Dad. We all head for the entrance.

Inside, the lobby is cool and inviting. I sit down between Riley and Mackenzie on a fish-shaped bench while Dad pulls our tickets out of his wallet and takes them up to the desk.

Mom goes over and takes the keys from Dad before joining us by the bench.

"Well, have fun, kids," she smiles.

"You aren't doing it with us, Mom?" I ask.

"Only four people can do it at a time, and they only do one dive a day," Mom explains. "Besides, I don't know how to swim. I'm going shopping."

"She'll enjoy that more than swimming with fish, anyway," Riley whispers to me when I start to protest.

Mom heads out the door again as Dad comes back over to our bench. A young guy dressed in a dark blue shirt and white pants follows him over.

"Hi, guys, I'm Rae," he says. Rae's enthusiasm is contagious, and I can't help but grin at him.

"So glad to hear you guys have signed up for the amazing experience of diving with sea creatures amidst the Great Maya Reef! We'll just head on over this way to those stairs over there and up to the Dive Room."

We follow Rae through the aquarium to a door that says *Maya Dive Experience.* Mackenzie grabs my hand and squeezes it excitedly.

Inside the Dive Room, we meet Erika Neil, one of the aquarium's Dive Volunteers. She gives a short presentation about the Maya Reef. It's the second largest in the world, and today, we get to see a small part of it. Then, she shows us our lockers- there's one with each of our names on it.

"Inside, you'll find wet suits and fins that have been pre-sized to the information that your Mom gave us," she explains. "I understand that this is a surprise for you guys?"

I nod. "I've never been snorkeling before."

"Don't worry," Erika smiles. "I'll teach you everything you need to know."

We all head into the change rooms and I take off my wig, and put on my swimming trunks and the wet suit. I've never worn a wet suit before, and it feels funny. The material is soft and stretchy, but as I close up the zipper in the back, it feels kind of tight.

When I get out of the change room, Mackenzie makes a funny face and grabs at the neck of her wet suit.

"I feel like I'm choking!" she says, pretending to gasp for breath.

Erika hears us and smiles. "Wet suits are meant to feel a little tight. It'll feel looser once you get in the water," she explains. She doesn't give a second glance at the fact that all our hair suddenly disappeared, and I love her for it.

Once we're all suited up, Erika leads us into the pool room. The large room has blue walls and random white pipes along the walls. It has a cavernous feel to it. Erika leads us onto a white plastic dock floating at the edge of the pool and gives us some snorkeling directions.

"Your fins might feel weird and cumbersome at first," she explains. "But once you get the hang of using them, they're great!"

Erika slips gracefully into the water. Riley's fins slide on the dock and he lands in the pool with a big splash. I grin and jump in after him. Mackenzie and Dad slide in the proper way.

I put the end of the snorkel tube in my mouth and duck my head underwater. Erika watches as we explore the pool.

Up top, the water looks dark and dreary, but underneath the surface it turns a beautiful shade of blue. Colourful angelfish and curious cownose rays swim around me. A school of parrot fish surrounds me, and it takes my breath away.

A bold cownose ray swims up to me, showing its white underbelly. Its mouth looks like it's curved into a smile. I reach a gentle hand out and slide it along the ray's back. It feels smooth and slippery.

Mackenzie swims over and grabs my hand and we go up for air. She spits out her snorkel.

"Did you see those tiny pink fish over by the big yellowish reef part?"

she asks excitedly. I shake my head. She pops her snorkel back in and pulls me under water.

We swim all over the reef, through hundreds of brilliantly coloured tropical fish. The water is just right, and I could stay down here for hours.

A clear tunnel runs through the pool, part of the aquarium's Great Maya Reef exhibit. I swim down to it and wave at the people walking through it.

As I glide through the artificial reef, it's like all the other worries slip away. It doesn't matter that leukemia could come back anytime, or that I still have a long way to go until the chance of relapse significantly lessens. It's just me and the fish and the water. And as far as surprises go, this is one of the best of my life.

All too soon, Erika motions us back to the surface, and we climb out of the pool.

"That was awesome!" Mackenzie says, eyes shining.

"I agree! Did you see that huge butterfly fish?" I ask, spreading my hands far apart to show how big it was.

Riley flips his wet hair up out of his eyes and grins. "There was a school of angelfish that swam right around me!" he says.

We head back to our change rooms and get out of the wetsuits. Erika thanks us for being such good students, and then we head out to the parking lot.

Mom is waiting for us in the SUV. The trunk is now full of packages and bags, and Dad asks Mom if she bought out the whole French Quarter.

"Of course not," Mom replies indignantly. "If I did that, there wouldn't be anything left for my *next* shopping spree.

"I'm starving," I call out as we exit the parking lot.

"There's a Cajun diner close by we could go to," Mom says. "We still have a few hours before we need to go to the train station."

"A *few*? More like six. It's only one-thirty," Riley yells from the backseat.

"It's called the 'Olde Nola Cookery'," Mom continues, as though she didn't hear Riley.

The Cookery isn't that far away, but Dad can't find parking right beside it, so we have to walk back half a block from a random parking lot in front of a live seafood restaurant. The Olde Nola Cookery is a small place on a busy street, sandwiched between a bar and a French restaurant. It's past the usual noon hour, but the place is still busy and we have to wait a few minutes for a table.

My stomach is growling by the time a waitress leads us to a table. I sit down on a golden oak chair beneath a large picture of a horse rearing in front of a lighthouse. Mackenzie flops down beside me.

"This place is cool," she says to me. "Look at the cool designs painted on the table."

"Just get me some *food* on this table," Riley groans as he picks up a menu.

The menu is typical Cajun seafood, and Mackenzie and I immediately go for the gator bites. I don't often get to eat alligator, but every time I do, I remember how good it is all over again. It tastes like a cross between chicken and fish, and it's super juicy. Mom just wrinkles her nose at us when our platter of alligator meat comes. She's got too much high society in her to stoop to even trying alligator.

Dad says a quick blessing for the food, and then we dig in.

"This is the best alligator I have ever tasted!" I exclaim after my first bite. Riley looks up from where he's stuffing his mouth with bayou duck.

"I doubt it's better than this duck," he teases.

"It doesn't even compare to our alligator," Mackenzie shoots back.

"That's cause it's so bad," Riley smirks.

"Can we *please* enjoy one family dinner without you three going at each other?" Mom sighs.

"We're just teasing each other," I say.

"Yah. It means we love each other," Riley adds.

Mom just rolls her eyes and turns back to her catfish platter.

We take our time eating lunch, but when we all pile back into the SUV, stuffed to the gills, we *still* have three hours to kill. Mom suggests shopping, and Dad says we had better go ride a ferry, or something where there aren't any stores for Mom to clean out.

"Let's go to the World War II Museum," Riley suggests.

"Nooo," Mackenzie and I chorus.

"We don't have time for that, Riley," Dad says.

"What about the New Orleans Museum of Art?" Mom suggests.

"Nooo!" all of us kids chorus.

"It's bad enough that you made us go to that art exhibit a few years ago," Riley adds.

"Yah. That one painting of a man sitting in a lemon scared me so bad I *still* have nightmares about it."

"You guys just don't appreciate fine art," Mom sniffs.

"You call a man sitting in a lemon *fine art*??!!" I exclaim.

"Okay, settle down everyone," Dad says. "How about we ride one of those old streetcars around town? There's one near here."

"Sure," Mackenzie says.

"That'd be better than an 'art' museum," Riley says, making air quotations as he says 'art'.

Dad stomps on the brakes and makes a quick right turn, causing three people to honk and a pedestrian to shake his fist at us.

"Almost missed the road," he laughs. "The streetcars are just down here."

Sure enough, a station is up ahead with a bright red, old-fashioned streetcar waiting for passengers. Dad quickly parks, and we hop on.

The rest of the afternoon passes uneventfully as we take in the sights and sounds of New Orleans. We eat a quick supper at McDonald's, despite Mom's protests, and head for the train station. We make it to the parking lot a minute before Grandpa and Grandma's train is due to arrive. Mom practically runs through the station to make it to the right terminal in time, but when we get there, Grandpa and Grandma are already off the platform and waiting. Grandma Charlton does not look happy.

"All those years of training you to be early, and you still can't even make it to a place on time," she snips at Mom as we greet them. Then she turns to us.

"Well, look at you two. They've lost weight, Carolina. I *told* you they need lots of carbs to get some fat back on their bones after their illness. A skinny girl doesn't make a pretty woman. Oh, and my, those shirts are bright. Young ladies shouldn't wear plaids. It looks boyish. And really, Carolina? You let them *match*? At their age?"

I give Mackenzie a sideways glance, and she grimaces back. It's going to be one long weekend.

7

Chapter 7

1849, June 28

Dear Diary,

It's been awhile since I've been able to write.

I finally moved this diary to a better spot down by our shack after Prissy's little brother, Arthur, almost caught me writing in it.

Our shacks are little wooden huts with dirt floors, down by the sugarcane fields. There are about twenty of them. My family's down near the end of the row. Sometimes I sleep on Prissy's floor in the Big House, but despite how homely our shack is, I'd much rather sleep here, snuggled up on the blanket between Rosie and Betsie,with Kitty at our feet.

Today Tom, Old George's son, got forty lashes.

I worry about Tom sometimes. He stands tall, and there is a sort of burning fire in his eyes. He refuses to be defeated in spirit. Sometimes I wish I was more like him -not so trodden down by white people- but it is a dangerous thing for a slave. Tom gets more lashes than anyone else, just because he refuses to bow his head and he stands straight and proud.

I really do wish I was more like him, but I am too much of a coward.
Nora Mae Washington

∞ ∞ ∞ ∞ ∞

Today we are going back to the hospital in New Orleans for more tests, to make sure the cancer is still gone. That's the thing about remission -you're glad to be better, yet sometimes you can hardly stand the dread of knowing that you can relapse at any moment.

Grandpa and Grandma Charlton left yesterday, thankfully, and some old friend of theirs who lives in nearby Labadieville volunteered to take them back to the station. I am *so* ready for a break from Grandma's constant criticisms. She is one of the hardest people to truly love.

The drive to New Orleans is quiet, and a little over an hour later, we pull up in front of the large complex of the New Orleans Children's Hospital.

I smooth my hands nervously over my pale pink sweatshirt. Beside me, Mackenzie is nervously fingering her hoodie sleeves.

And this is only one of the many follow-up appointments.

Mom places a hand on each of our backs and guides us to reception. Dr. Lindsey meets us in the waiting room, her long dark hair pulled back into a low ponytail. The woman who has essentially helped save our lives gives us a smile and leads us to the elevator.

"We'll head up to the Cancer Wing and go from there," she explains.

Mackenzie presses the all-too-familiar button in the elevator- Floor Five. A few seconds later, the door opens again with a soft hiss.

The waiting area in the Pediatric Cancer Wing is brightly colored, with pictures and drawings all over the walls. Over in one corner sits a white wall with hundreds of names written on it. A big yellow bell hangs on a rope from the ceiling above the wall. Inscribed on the side of the bell is one word: *hope.*

"Let's go find our name!" I whisper to Mackenzie after Dr. Lindsey seats us in the waiting room.

She grabs my hand. Her fingers are ice cold.

I run my eyes over the names written in colorful ink, searching for two in purple.

"There it is!" Mackenzie whispers, laying her finger on two names written in bold letters.

'Taylor and Mackenzie Everett

May 7, 2022'

I whisper the names under my breath.

Just then a blonde nurse comes over.

"Taylor and Mackenzie, we're ready for you," she said in a kind voice.

Mackenzie shoots me a nervous look as we follow Nurse Emily into the room.

The large blue room holds two beds, and there are hot air balloons on the border. But it looks way too much like the room where Mackenzie and I laid side-by-side as the chemo drugs dripped slowly into our veins.

Nurse Emily helps me up on the one bed while Mom helps Mackenzie up on the other one. The thin mattresses are hard and cold- definitely not made with comfort as a top priority.

Dr. Lindsey breezes in just then. She's wearing pretty baby blue scrubs today, and they make her eyes shine. Or maybe her eyes always shine; she's just that kind of person

"We don't normally use this room for examinations like this, but we wanted the sisters to be together," she explains, flashing a smile. I grin back, grateful for her thoughtfulness. Mom sits down nervously in the chair in the corner. That chair probably holds as many bad memories for her as the beds do for me and Mackenzie.

Dr. Lindsey starts by doing a physical exam, checking my liver, spleen, and lymph nodes for abnormal swelling. She keeps up a steady patter of distracting chit chat while she works. She thinks our prank on our friends is hilarious, and can't hold back a grin at my retelling of Mackenzie being a Holstein dog.

She is surprised that we've been attending school and parties. "The effects of chemo usually last for nearly a month!" she exclaims. "You two should have been bed-ridden!"

"Well we didn't get to ring the bell until almost three weeks after our last chemo," Mackenzie reminds the doctor, "and we were in the hospital for a couple days right after, too. Remember? Our white blood cell counts were off and you panicked like a cat in a dog park and tied us up all over again."

Dr. Lindsay just grins. "I had to make sure my favourite patients were alright."

"I bet you tell *all* your patients that," I retort good-naturedly.

"Oh, but I have some *favourite* favourites.

"Sounds like you two got to return to your normal lives after ringing the bell. You got over all the side effects while in the hospital!" Nurse Emily puts in.

I don't tell her of sleeping fifteen hours at a time those first few days home, or almost barfing at school on Monday. No doubt the doctor would have accused Mom of letting us loose too early.

Nurse Emily swabs my arm in the bend of my elbow. "We're just going to take some blood for some tests," she explains calmly.

I stare up at the white ceiling as she pricks my arm. Mackenzie likes to watch them stick her, but I just can't. It doesn't really hurt, but watching the needle pierce my skin just makes me squeamish.

"And... done," Nurse Emily says, slapping a square of gauze on my arm. Five vials of my blood lie on her tray.

Dr. Lindsey leads me to the X-ray room while Nurse Emily takes Mackenzie's blood. I lay down on the familiar hard bench while the X-ray machine whirs around above me. I shut my eyes tight. "Please, God, don't let the cancer have come back!" I silently pray.

Soon it's over, and I head back to the exam room to wait for my sister.

When Mackenzie comes back, the doctor shuts the door and sits down. "The blood test results should be back by the end of the week," she explains. "We'll call with the results of those and the X-rays, then, as well as the CBC. All the organs look good for both of you, though." She gives us a bright smile.

I clench my hands in my lap. One whole week to not know whether you have cancer or not, and this is only the beginning.

∞ ∞ ∞ ∞ ∞

On Friday, I wake up feeling nauseous.

"Mac," I whisper, "I don't feel good."

She shoots me a worried look.

"How do you feel?" she asks.

"Like I usually did after chemo," I groan. "Can you still feel the effects after over a month?"

Mackenzie shrugs. "Probably. It's strong stuff. It's literally chemicals that are strong enough to make your hair fall out."

I roll over and go back to sleep almost immediately. By noon, I wake up feeling as perky as ever. I just hope it isn't a sign of the cancer returning.

It turns out, I have nothing to worry about. That afternoon, Mackenzie and I were reading in the library when we got a call from the hospital. "All your tests came back clear!" Mom yells to us.

I grab Mackenzie and we do an impromptu dance in the lounge. Mamie comes running from the kitchen and gives us each a floury hug. Even Rachel stops the cleaning to give us a thumbs up.

We're still cancer free.

Yet we still have a long way to go. The leukemia could easily come back, especially in the first two years. And we aren't out of remission for another five years. Besides, the cancer could still come back any time during our lives. Somedays, it feels like leukemia is sitting on my shoulder, just waiting to strike again.

It's hard to live, sometimes, when you know that kind of stuff.

Mom asks the doctor about my earlier sickness, but Dr. Lindsey says it was probably just the treatments coming through.

I sigh in relief.

III

July

Some of the best memories are made in flip-flops.
-unknown

8

Chapter 8

The summer breeze ripples the bunting and banners in the back garden. Mamie, Rachel, and Rebecca hurry to and fro with fried chicken, lemonade, and sweet potatoes.

All the Everett cousins are over, from eighteen-year-old Reid right on down to Baby Layla.

Mackenzie nudges me in the side and whispers, "Imagine if this was the Turner's. Everyone would be decked out in suits and gowns in this heat."

I snicker. "And we'd probably have to play charades and tell our cousins all about our little dog's antics."

Mom overhears us and raises an eyebrow.

"The Turners may be different, but different isn't necessarily bad."

"It's bad when all your parties include ballroom dancing," Riley says behind us. He was unfortunate enough to be invited to one of those last year. Mackenzie and I got out of it by being in the hospital.

Mom rolls her eyes and gives us her famous 'what-do-I-do-with-you-now' look. "God still calls us to love the Turner's," she finally says.

A shriek sounds from over by the oaks. Nine-year-old Simon is chasing Julia and Meghan around with a toad.

Riley runs over to the ruckus. He grabs the toad and stuffs it down Simon's shirt front. Simon dances around, yelling, as the toad jumps around inside his shirt, trying to escape.

Meghan and Julia act like Riley's the hero of the hour- which, I guess, to them he is- and Mackenzie is doubled over beside me, the sunshine glinting off her short, dark waves.

Our hair is finally growing back again, so we decided to deck it out with red, white, and blue bows. It's the Fourth of July, and to me, it's the best day in the whole summer.

Uncle John clears his throat just then. Nobody can clear their throat as loud as Uncle John, so he's the designated attention-getter in the family. Everyone quiets down and circles around the stone patio at the back of the house. Dad waits while Mamie finishes setting the last platter of food down, then steps to the center of the patio. Then he opens a paper and begins to read the Everett Family Declaration of Independence. *"We believe that all men were created by God as equal and free...We believe we are privileged and blessed to be born in a free country, but by no means a superior people...For our kingdom is in Heaven, and not on this earth...We will always remember the sacrifices of the faithful who have gone on before us..."*

I give a little sigh. As much as I am thankful to be born in such a strong, solid family, the reading of the Family Declaration is loooong, especially when you're hungry.

"But above all and through all, we firmly stand and live by the Biblical truth."

Dad finishes reading it and Charlie echoes, "Amen." The family declaration was created by my Great-Grandpa Everett during the Civil War. Although he had slaves under his care, he believed in paying them a wage and providing for them so they had decent food and living conditions. During his time, Grandpa rescued over two hundred slaves from auctions and gave them free papers. We read it every Fourth of July to remember the legacy we have been given.

Then we sing the national anthem together, with Aunt Lynn accompanying us on her guitar. Finally Dad bows his head to bless the food.

"Dear Lord our Father, we thank You for Your rich mercies and the many blessings you have given us. Thank you for family, and for friends..."

After his lengthy prayer, I rush with the rest of the kids to the food tables. I am *starving*.

After lunch, Mackenzie and I take our younger cousins -all sixteen of them- up to our room to see all the hats and wigs we've collected. When we open up our 'wig-drawer', they all kind of 'ooh' and 'aah'.

Simon thinks it's hilarious that his two older girl cousins have hair as short as his own, and five-year-old Maisie tries to steal the auburn wig. We let the girls take a few of the wigs in the end. They mostly choose the neon ones or the wigs that remind them of Disney princesses. Despite my fears, our cancer really is gone right now, so we might as well start living like it.

In the evening we all pile into Uncle William's limo. He redid an old hearse that he happened to buy at a garage sale into a limo, and we can stuff the whole family in there. Then we drive to Thibodaux for the fireworks. On the drive there, as per tradition, Uncle William recounts the story of how he secured his old hearse limo.

"Well, now, I was out driving yer Aunt Becky 'round town an' we was lookin' at garage sales. She was hopin' to buy a crockpot, an' I was lookin' fer tools."

Uncle William has the most atrocious English of anyone I know, but it kind of fits him. He's the kind of guy that English teachers use as examples- the *bad* examples. But he's a great guy, despite his English, and he can spin a tale like no one else I know.

"Well, we pull up to the drive of an older guy. We hadn'a had much luck yet, an' we been goin' half 'o' the mornin'. We was gettin' real discouraged. All I'd found was a hammer with a chewed up handle, and yer Aunt Becky hadn'a found nothin' at all! Anyways, we pull up there, and this old fellar comes hobblin' up as we browse and we talk a l'il, y'know, about crops an' weather, an' his grand kids. An' than all of a sudden, right out 'o' the blue, he up an' says, 'by any chance, would you like a hearse?' An' I says, 'well now, don't reckon I *need* one, cuz I ain't got no funeral home or a death in the family, but I'd sure *like* one!' An' he leads me out back, an' there's a big, black, solid hunk o' steel on wheels, and he says he used to drive it to work across town at the diner, but he's retired now, an' since it doesn't fit in his parking space at church, he doesn't really use it. An' I said I'll take it, and he says it's all mine for five hundred dollars. And that's how yer Uncle William got a hearse. An' I jest tore out the stuff in the back that needed to be taken out an' reupholstered the seats from funeral black to a classy gray, an' there ya' go- the Everett family hearse- sorry, limo."

Uncle William's story is always the perfect length to get us from my house to the park in Thibodaux, and he pulls into the parking lot as he finishes it up.

The parking lot is swamped.It seems like the whole town has shown up at the park for the fireworks.

Julia and Meghan snuggle on the blanket beside Mackenzie and I. And as I lie on my back with the colorfulness exploding in the sky above, I can't help thinking, "Man, it's good to be alive!"

∞ ∞ ∞ ∞ ∞

1849, July 4

Massa and Missy Andrews have taken the whole family to town for the Fourth of July, so we're all heading back to a little clearing in the woods even though it's not Sunday, to have church.

By law, we get every Sunday off 'for worship,' and although Old George says we should be allowed to hold church, Massa Andrews forbids it. I guess he thinks slaves don't deserve to be spiritually uplifted, or maybe he's just too scared it'll give us power and courage.

But on Sundays, when Massa Andrews takes his family to church, we all go back to a secluded clearing in the woods. Just because we're slaves don't mean we don't need God. And we will endure anything to meet with Him.

My papa is the preacher because he can read, so he reads from the New Testament Old George has.

Papa taught me to read as a little girl, even though it's dangerous for a slave. He wanted me to feel that much more human, and to always remember I'm somebody, not just Massa Andrew's property, or Prissy's 'dog' or whatever else she wants me to be.

I wonder about this Independence Day. It's to celebrate freedom, but I'm not free. Is freedom only for white people? Will the world ever get to the point where skin doesn't matter, and people with skin like fresh milk can celebrate beside people with skin the colour of hot cocoa? These are things I wonder sometimes, late at night when I'm lying on our pallet.

The world is a hard place for a girl like me, but for once I have a bit of good news, too. Tom, who works in the stable, and is Massa Andrew's driver because he is so good-looking, gave me a metal box the other day. It has a lock on it, and a small key on a gold chain. He says he found it in the stable trash.

I just hope he didn't steal it.

I lock my diary in there, now. It keeps the paper dry. And since it protects the diary against the elements, I moved it back to the church clearing so's no one finds it in my hut. That could bring punishment on my whole family.

I keep the key hidden under a tree root. It is too dangerous to wear it. But it feels good to finally have something worth protecting, and something with which to protect it.

Nora Mae Washington

9

Chapter 9

Riley got his full license now. He's almost seventeen, and can finally drive all by himself!

So Mackenzie got this idea that we should go to the library and try to find out more about Nora Mae Washington. And Riley can drive us there.

I wonder where Nora May lived. Did she live at our place? But Great-grandpa Everett owned the plantation, not a "Massa Andrews," right? How did her diary end up in the clearing in our woods? And what about those shackles? There are so many questions, and never enough answers.

Since Riley is eager to drive places, it isn't hard to convince him to take us to town. He drops us off at the library and leaves to meet some friends.

"Be back in half an hour," he calls. We wave to him and enter the library.

The Thibodaux Library is cool and quiet. The bookshelves are dark wood, and floral patterned, vintage chairs are scattered around. Books of all shapes, colours, and sizes line the shelves.

"Hello, ladies," the librarian says in a soft voice, smiling at us over her black cat-eye glasses. "How can I help you?"

"Hi, we're looking for some history on our property," I reply. "From back in the mid 1800s or so."

"Mmm, just go to Aisle D. We have logs of property records dating back to the 1700s. You may also look at old newspapers using the microfilm if you wish," she directs.

Mackenzie and I race to Aisle D. Long rows of rich brown, leather-covered books lie on the shelves. There is one for every year since 1785. We quickly find the book for 1849 and carefully open it. I peer over my sister's shoulder as we scan the index.

"What parish are we in?" she asks. "These books cover the whole state of Louisiana!"

We find our parish, or as they call them in some places, 'county', in the large book. There is an index of landowners for each parish, too. I skimmed my fingers down the list. "There! Andrews!" I cry.

"But there are three of them!" Mackenzie protests. "Joseph Andrews, William Andrews, and St. Clair Andrews."

I shrug. "That's not too bad. Let's look at them all," I suggest.

Joseph Andrews owned a flour mill in Thibodaux, so he couldn't be the one. Besides, he's listed as a Quaker, and they didn't support slavery. St. Clair Andrews had a sugarcane plantation, but he had all sons; no Priscilla Andrews there.

Mackenzie turns the page. A map is spread out on the paper.

"Wait, isn't that our place?" I whisper incredulously. According to the map, a creek flows from behind the house and meanders through the property, just like at our place. Where we have pastures, though, it has fields of cotton and sugarcane, but the woods and hollows are all in the right places.

"It is!" Mackenzie cries, "and look!" She runs her finger over the list of William Andrews' family and slaves.

William Andrews Oct. 19, 1802

Catherine Andrews May 21, 1810

Children:

Priscilla K. Andrews June 3, 1835

Anthony L. Andrews Jan. 7-16, 1837

Julia M. Andrews Mar. 11, 1839

Sarah J. Andrews Apr. 11, 1842

Mitchell I. Andrews Apr. 17, 1844

Noah I. Andrews Apr. 17, 1844

"It's definitely them," I say, "and there's Nora Mae!" There she was, under her father and mother's names.

"She was only thirteen," Mackenzie whispers sadly.

"But I thought Great-grandpa Everett had the land back then," I say, puzzled.

"Well, let's check more books," my sister answers eagerly.

I pull out a book from 1852 while Mackenzie tries an even later year. "He owned it in 1867," she says.

"... but not in 1852," I finish. "So we need to work towards the middle of those years."

Slowly we work through the large volumes of each year in between. "I found it!" I cry a few minutes later. "Great-grandpa Everett bought the land from William Andrews in 1858, including all the slaves."

"So he bought Nora Mae?" Mackenzie asks eagerly.

I shake my head. "No, she's not listed here. I haven't seen her in any of the records since 1850."

"I wonder what happened to her," Mackenzie says as we put the books back.

"Maybe she escaped to Canada," I suggest.

"Maybe," Mackenzie replies, a little doubtfully. "We'll just have to keep reading her diary, I guess."

We thank the librarian and sit on the front steps to wait. I watch idly as a young mother across the street tries to keep her son from eating a stick. Soon Riley pulls up in his blue sports car.

Mackenzie climbs into the back seat while I sit up front. Riley tosses us each a coke, and we roar away towards home.

◯◯ ◯◯ ◯◯ ◯◯ ◯◯

July 10,1849

Dear Diary,

Old George is now the driver for Massa Andrews. Massa has decided that he can get more work out of Tom than Old George, and George makes a rather distinguished looking driver with his salt and pepper hair and wise face.

Tom sure ain't happy to be out in the fields, though. He always thought he was better'n that. I worry more about him every day.

I reckon by now, if anyone ever reads this, they might be thinking I've got feelings for Tom, so I may as well admit that I do. I admire his fire and sense of justice. He's also real handsome, and gentle with all the little young'uns and babies, and the older folks. Although, he's five years older than me, and most likely doesn't think twice 'bout me, but it doesn't hurt to dream. I guess that's why his spit and fire worries me so much. I'd be devastated if something happened to him.

Rosie's sick with a flu, even though it's middle summer, but there ain't much we can do. Massa Andrews won't call a doctor for a black young'un, and Mama and I gotta work in the Big House all day, so there's only Old Ida to look out for her. I know what's really wrong with Rosie. The small wrinkly potatoes and beans we get aren't enough for her to grow. Papa says she needs more meat.

Yesterday was church back in the clearing again. Papa told the story of the Israelites' escape from Egypt. After that, Tom and some of the other folks were muttering of running off to Canada.

As much as I want to be free, I know how risky it is to run away. Massa

Andrews will set his dogs after you, and you can't outrun or out smell a dog. Then you'll just get a whipping and either die or get sold, probably to some worse-off place.

I know there's some who done it, and there's white folks who don't believe in slavery and help them, but just as many get caught, then whipped or even shot to death.

Working in the Big House is brutal right now. Missy Andrews is planning another party, so we've got to get the house all perfect. Prissy makes me try about near five different hairdo's every day. Aunt Lyla is working fiercely to get new gowns done.

Aunt Lyla is the Andrews's seamstress. Missy says she's the best sewer around, even if she is black. Of course she doesn't say that to Aunt Lyla's face, so I make sure to tell her what I overhear.

My own dress is a brown thread-bare garment, but Prissy says I might get a new one from her scraps so the slaves will look good at the party. The minister's wife is coming, so the Andrews must put on a good face, even towards the slaves.

I'm so tired of being a slave. I'm someone else's property, and they control my every move. I can read and write good, but no one can know. Even my name isn't my own.

I know these are dangerous thoughts for a slave, but I think them anyway. Nora Mae Washington

∞ ∞ ∞ ∞ ∞

The night is clear and warm. There isn't a cloud in the sky, and the moon is faint. The stars shine brightly overhead as I attempt to haul myself and a blanket up the ladder.

Down below, Riley jiggles the ladder a little, and I give a little yelp. He laughs, so I look down and shine my headlamp in his eyes for a second. He blinks furiously and looks away.

"Are you trying to kill me?" I ask him.

"Nah, just hurry up. You're climbing a ladder, not walking a tightrope."

"Well, then, you can carry this blanket up," I retort.

"Hey, I wasn't the one who said I need a blanket to go stargazing. You can take your *own-*"

"Come on, guys, I found the perfect spot!" Mackenzie yells from halfway across the roof. I quickly scramble the remainder of the way up the ladder and onto the roof.

The roof of our house is relatively steep on the sides, but unlike some houses, our antebellum-era mansion doesn't have a peak on top-instead, it has a little flat area. There are also little nooks and crannies made by the attic dormer windows that are good places to sit. Mackenzie is spreading her blanket on the tippy-top of the roof, and I hurry over as carefully as I can. I can hear Riley scrambling up the long ladder behind me.

My bare feet grip the rough shingles. Dad only lets us do this if there's like no chance of rain. Slipping on this roof would send you on a deadly plunge three stories down. I climb up to the flat part and spread my blanket down beside Mackenzie's.

"Look, there's the Big Dipper!" Mackenzie says, pointing up at the stars. I lean back and try to find it as Riley climbs up beside us.

"Man these shingles are cold," he says as he lies down beside me.

"That's why I brought a blanket," I tell him as I turn my headlamp off. He sticks his tongue out at me. I let him shiver for a few minutes before moving over and letting him share the blanket.

Riley and I locate the Big Dipper, soon, and trace the pointer stars in the 'cup' to the Little Dipper.

"See that really bright star up there in the Little Dipper?" Riley asks. "That's Polaris, or the North Star. It's special, because it's really bright, and it never seems to move."

"Slaves used to follow it to get to Canada," I add, thinking of the diary. I wonder if Nora Mae ever followed that star to freedom.

"I see the rest of the Big Bear- you know, that constellation that the Big Dipper's in!" Mackenzie says excitedly. I lean my head next to hers and try to follow her pointing finger.

"I don't...oh, I think I see it!" I say, tracing the shape out with my hand.

"And there's Cassiopeia!" Mackenzie says after a few minutes. She always was the best at finding constellations.

A cool breeze blows over us, and we huddle together. No one is ready to climb down yet, no matter how cold it is. There's something magical about a velvety sky full of sparkling stars.

"It feels so huge," I whisper.

"I know," Mackenzie whispers back. "And yet God made it just by saying a few words."

"Kinda makes you feel small, y'know?" Riley says.

"It sure is better than those glow in the dark stars they had on the ceiling in our hospital room," Mackenzie giggles. "And those didn't make constellations."

It's quiet then, except for the rush of the breeze and the chattering of our teeth. Finally Riley breaks the silence.

"I went up here one time last summer when you two were sick. I couldn't understand why God didn't heal you guys, and why I was the healthy one. I was just staring up at the sky, talking with- okay, kind of yelling at- God, and all of a sudden the North Star just jumped out at me. And this thought just went through my head that, 'God's like that star'. Sometimes He's hard to see, but He always stays the same, just like how the North Star never seems to move, and He's happy to give you direction."

I put an arm around Riley's shoulders and give them a squeeze. Then I think about what he said all the way down the ladder and up to my bed, and before I fall asleep, I say a little 'thank you' prayer to God for being the North Star.

10

Chapter 10

Our birthday is next week, and the whole house is caught in an uproar about it.

Last year I celebrated my birthday in the hospital. This year I just got my July check-up results back: I'm still all clear. Mackenzie is, too.

Rachel is busy cleaning the house from top to bottom, her light blonde hair tied up in a kerchief. Rebecca is sprucing up all the gardens, her light brown hands busily churning the dirt and pulling weeds. Mamie practically lives in the kitchen nowadays, and Charlie and Thomas are helping Dad and Riley wash down and decorate the stable.

The Sunday before our birthday even the preacher shakes our hands and says, "Happy Birthday."

I guess when you might not have more birthdays, it becomes a big deal. Or when you have a brush with death, your birthdays become that much more special.

The day before our birthday, Mom shoos us out of the house for the final preparations. Mackenzie and I decide to take the gator back to the woods to explore the clearing a bit more. We head back through the pastures to the bush, laughing and singing while the sun warms our arms and hair. I tip my head back and take a good, long look at the brilliant blue sky before we head into the dark forest.

We cut a better trail through the brush to the clearing. We bounce over a few rocks and narrowly miss a tree in the process.

I laugh at Mackenzie as we bounce over a mound of dirt. "Are you sure you know how to drive this thing?"

She glares at me and almost gets hung up on a tree stump.

Finally we break out into the clearing. I step down into the tall grass and weeds. The metal shackles are still in the clearing by the stone platform.

Stuck in a crevice of the platform we find a strip of leather with a gold embossed

'HO

BI'

"It's the Bible they preached from!" Mackenzie cries. Its pages had long since rotted away, but the leather strip had been sheltered in the stone.

I look around the dark clearing. A chill goes up my spine. It's eerie to think that almost two hundred years ago another girl close to our age was having church in this same clearing on a slave plantation.

Then my breath catches in my throat. I grab Mackenzie's arm.

"Look! Is that..."

Mackenzie gasps beside me.

Half-protruding out of the dirt is the dirty, bony structure of a skull. An empty eye socket stares lifelessly up at the sky.

I turn away and gag.

"Let's get out of here!" Mackenzie screams.

We run back to the gator as fast as we can, and I throw it in forward. We roar around in a circle and bounce out of there, trying to comprehend what we have just come across on our property.

∞ ∞ ∞ ∞ ∞

1849, July 22

Dear Diary,

Today Massa Andrews called us all up to the Big House. Overnight, Tom and another fellow, Big Jim, ran away. Massa asked us lots of questions about them; then he searched our huts himself. I'm glad Tom gave me that metal box to hide my diary in, or Massa mighta found it for sure.

Of course we all knew Tom and Big Jim ran away. They asked us all if anyone else wanted to come with them. But we all just played dumb, which isn't very hard to do when your Massa sees you as little more than a cow or a horse anyway.

I hope and pray that Tom and Big Jim make it to Canada. And maybe someday, I can, too.

Nora Mae Washington

∞ ∞ ∞ ∞ ∞

The morning of our birthday dawns clear and bright, but I still feel a little sick to the stomach after seeing that skull.

Mackenzie tried to reason that it probably wasn't even a human skull, but we both know how easily it *could* be one.

Allie, Ellie, and Remy are coming over for the afternoon and a birthday supper, but Mom says there is a surprise for us in the morning. She tells us to dress up in decent clothes, then refuses to say more.

I pull out my favourite striped cowgirl shirt and toss a matching one to Mackenzie. We don't often twin, but today seems like the perfect day to do it.

Downstairs Mom ties blindfolds over our eyes, and Riley leads us out to the SUV. "Where are we going?" Mackenzie giggles, clutching my hand. Excited butterflies dance around in my stomach.

"Just wait and see," Dad calls out mysteriously from the driver's seat.

I buckle up and try to ignore the excited jitters that insist on continuing in my stomach.

We drive about fifteen minutes, then pull over and stop. Dad and Riley help us out of the SUV and across uneven ground.

I feel Dad lift me in the air and set me on a corrugated surface. "Easy there," I hear someone say. It sounds like Mayor Francis, but I have no idea why the mayor would be here. It's just a birthday.

Riley helps us sit down, then Mom tells us we can take our blindfolds off. We are sitting in the box of a red pick up. Dad and Mom are standing on the ground beside us. Mayor Francis *is* there, after all. I shoot Mackenzie a confused look. She just shrugs.

"What's the sur..." I start to ask, but Dad cuts me off with a raised hand.

"Just wait and see," he says mysteriously. Dad and Mom jump in the cab with the mayor, while Riley sits in the box with us. We enter the outskirts of Thibodaux. Up ahead on Main Street, I can see the flashing red and blue lights of a cop car.

"Uh-oh. If that's a cop, we're in trouble," Mackenzie whispers. "I don't think riding in a truck box is legal."

I squirmed uncertainly. But the cop just waves at us and motions for us to follow him.

People are crowded on the sidewalks up ahead. I feel like ducking down in the truck bed. Why am I riding down Main Street in a truck bed, anyway? A cheer rises up in the crowd as we near. People begin raising signs and banners.

Suddenly I catch on.

"Mac! It's a birthday parade for us!" I squeal, pointing to a sign.

"Happy 14th Mackenzie and Taylor," it reads.

Another sign says, "Fourteen Years Strong!"

I can't believe it.

It seems that everybody and their mother's brother is there. I recognize school friends, my dentist, teachers, doctors and nurses from

New Orleans, and even the librarian with the cat-eye glasses.

"Are all these people celebrating us?"Mackenzie asks incredulously.

"Yup," Riley grins.

My smile is so big it feels like my face is splitting in two. I lean over the side of the pickup truck and just wave.

The mayor leads us up and down Main Street four times, led by the cop car. Finally, we stop at the end of the street.

People come swarming over. They hand us cards, flowers, candy, and good wishes as we kneel in the truck bed. There are so many people;it's just a blur. I don't remember who I've all talked to, and how many times I've said 'thank you'. I do feel tears pricking the back of my eyelids at the extreme show of love, though.

I can see tears streaming down Mom's face as she sticks her head out the window. The cop gives us his megaphone, and Mackenzie and I take turns giving a big thanks to the crowds gathered around the truck. And they're all there for us.

After a while, the crowds step back, and Lauren, Ellie, and Remy jump into the box with us. The cop car escorts us back to the SUV. Cards cover almost the entire truck box floor. Mackenzie and I each have an armful of flowers and enough chocolate to give a diabetes specialist a heart attack.

I don't realize I am crying until Riley lays his arm across my shoulders and wipes a finger under my eyes. He's got tears in his eyes, too.

When you're alive, people really love you, but I guess when you almost die, people really *show* you they love you.

We even get a card from Evangeline.

oo oo oo oo oo

The red Toyota, with Charlie at the wheel, pulls into the driveway right after us. All of the servants pile out.

"Mamie, guess what!" I cry.

She laughs. "Oh, I was there, child. Wouldn't have missed it for the world. Now let's go get some cake into you girls."

Mamie is so excited about her cake that she can hardly sit still during the main course. And when she finally brings it out, I can see why.

It's covered in a smooth layer of grassy green fondant. Silver fondant horseshoes spill down the side. On top, two icing horse heads look very much like Stormy and Oakley.

"Oh," Mackenzie breathes.

I'm speechless. I could only imagine the hours of work Mamie put into it.

"I love it!" I finally whisper. It was so cool I don't want to cut it, but Mamie shows no such hesitation. She grabs her biggest cake knife and cuts us each a generous slice from the three-tiered cake.

I pick a horseshoe off my piece and munch on it. It isn't fondant after all, but a hard, sugary candy.

"Made 'em myself, I did," Mamie says proudly.

"It's delicious," I assure her.

Each horseshoe is carefully and individually painted with food paint. They're a work of art all in themselves.

Allie munches on Stormy's eye. "This is a good cake, Mamie!" she exclaims.

Mamie beams.

After lunch we set to work in the lounge, opening and reading dozens of cards.

There are cards from classmates, neighbors, and the whole police force. And best of all, there are cards from other kids, just like us, in the New Orleans Hospital with cancer.

"Dear Everett twins,

I'm Lula and I'm five. I have had cancer for two years now. I hope you have a happy birthday," I read.

"Hey, look, this one's from the governor of Louisiana!" Mackenzie cries. "How did they get that pulled off?"

"And here's one from the fire team in Thibodaux," Ellie yells.

The one from Evangeline, who we haven't seen since her disastrous birthday party, assures us that Princess is doing fine, and she'll never forget Mackenzie's one-of-a-kind Holstein dog performance.

Boy, do we feel loved.

11

Chapter 11

1849, July 28

Well, Tom got away, but they caught Big Jim.

There have been signs posted all over town this past week, and posters with their faces on, and Massa Andrews hired some slave catchers with dogs to track Tom and Big Jim.

Yesterday they came riding in. Big Jim was bruised and bleeding, shackled on a rope behind the one horse. But the worst was his eyes. They had an absolutely defeated look about them, as though hope had been crushed beyond repair. And maybe, in a way, for Big Jim it had. He tasted freedom, and then it got taken away from him so fast.

Tom got away, but the slave catchers are going out after him, again. They tried to get information out of Big Jim, but thankfully Tom didn't tell him where he was going next.

Massa made us all watch as Big Jim was tied to a tree and whipped 'til he couldn't stand no more, and then some.

Massa Andrews says to let this be an example to us.

Old Ida knows some plant potions for sicknesses and things, so she takes care of Big Jim's back. It's a bloody mess, and Ida says she just hopes he don't get infected.

Massa's foreman has been keeping a closer eye on us down by the huts. Rosie's still sick, but it's harder to sneak her scraps from the Big House now, like me and Kitty used to do. She's at the point where Massa don't even make her work in the sugar house no more, cause she just can't. I worry 'bout her ev'ry day.

I wonder if life will always be this way for black people. Will we always be slaves? Will we always struggle for the basic necessities?

Nora Mae Washington

◌◌ ◌◌ ◌◌ ◌◌ ◌◌

"I'm bored!" Mackenzie groans, flopping down on the couch.

I idly flip through channels on the TV. The craze of our birthday party has come and gone, and now it seems there is nothing to do.

The heat outside is almost unbearable, but there isn't much to do inside, either. We can't ride horses, because Oakley is lame in one leg and Stormy won't ride very far without her, and besides, they'd probably get heatstroke.

I flip past a karate show in Korean, and a skinny man demonstrating how to do a back flip, then sigh. "Only a month till school," I remind my sister. Mackenzie rolls her eyes up to the ceiling.

"I can't survive a whole month of doing nothing," she complains.

We leave the TV and wander upstairs to the kitchen. Mamie is at the counter, punching down bread dough. She looks up at us. Sweat shines on her dark brow in the warm room. "What's with the long faces, girls?" she asks us.

"We're bored," Mackenzie sighs. I flop down on a stool at the breakfast bar.

Mamie laughs "I wish *I* had that problem." Then she smiles at us mysteriously. "Enjoy it while it lasts," is all she says.

I give Mackenzie a look. She just shrugs and follows me out to the lounge. My cell phone rings as I plop down on the couch. The caller ID says *Turner* and I stifle a groan.

"Hello," I say, hoping it isn't another party invitation.

"Hello, this is Mrs. Turner." Mrs. Turner sounds worried and I've never heard her talk so fast. I struggle to understand as she rushes on.

"I'm on the way to the hospital. Evangeline broke her leg, and I was wondering if I could drop Princess off for the night? Evangeline would feel so much better if her friends could take care of Princess. She doesn't want the poor little dog to be home alone while she's in the hospital."

I shoot Mackenzie a look. First of all, when did we join Evangeline's 'friends' list? I thought she barely tolerated us. Also, how did Mrs. Turner let her get up high enough to break a leg?

Mackenzie is waving her hands, trying to get my attention. "What? What?" she keeps mouthing at me. I ignore her and tell Mrs. Turner that we will take the dog. It's only one night, after all.

I get off the phone and tell Mackenzie what we have just gotten ourselves into. Her eyes get a little big and she says, "What if we kill the dog? You already poisoned it once."

"That was an *accident*," I retort back.

I go find Mom out on the back patio, reading, and tell we have acquired a house dog for the night. She just raises an eyebrow at me and says, "Well, she's your responsibility."

About fifteen minutes later, Mrs. Turner is at our door, looking harried and carrying a large pink crate and a mound of supplies.

"I have to go to the hospital now," she says. She hands us a binder titled *The Care and Keeping of Princess*, and unloads the pile of dog accessories on the porch. "If you have any questions, you have my number," she calls over her shoulder as she hurries back to her Porsche. Then she's gone in a cloud of dust.

Mackenzie and I look at each other, surrounded by a big fluffy bed, a stand with three bowls on it, an assortment of leashes and coats, and one little Yorkie.

"Well," Mackenzie finally says, "I guess we have something to do, now."

For some reason, that sends us into a fit of giggles, and we laugh all the way upstairs to our room, lugging Princess' stuff with us.

We sit on my bed and unload Princess from her carrier. She quickly picks her favourite- me- and settles down on my lap. Mackenzie opens the pink binder and starts reading.

"Princess has supper in her *light pink* bowl, water in her *dark pink* bowl, and treats in her *white* bowl," Mackenzie reads. "She gets two treats a day- one at ten and one at two. Princess may <u>only</u> have *Ray's* brand Salmon Chunk Treats, and must have exactly <u>4 oz.</u> of *Ray's* brand Chicken Veggie Stew wet food at 8 am and 4pm." Mackenzie looks up from the binder and gives me a look.

"Taylor, whyyyy did you say yes?" she moans.

I grin at her. "Well, remember what the preacher said on Sunday about loving your enemies?"

Mackenzie flops back on my bed. "Why does it have to be so hard?" she groans.

We play with Princess for most of the afternoon, not because we really love the dog, but because we need something to do. Before we know it, Mom is calling us to the supper table.

Mamie has prepared us a delicious meal of maple-glazed salmon and new potatoes, and I dig in heartily. My appetite is back in full force, and I can even manage to get a full plate down, now, unlike our first home meal.

Dad clears his throat and lays down his fork in the middle of the main course. He leans towards us. "Girls," he begins, "your mother and I were thinking. You two are getting a little bored around here, so we were wondering if you two would enjoy two weeks at summer camp."

I shoot a delighted look at my twin sister.

"That would be so much fun," I exclaim.

Dad holds up his hand. "The camp is... for kids with cancer." He adds, "We thought you might want to meet other kids your age who've been through the same stuff."

Everyone falls silent. Finally Mackenzie speaks up. "It's not gonna be just a glorified hospital, is it?" she asks uncertainly.

Dad smiles and shakes his head. "Oh no. It's 100% summer camp, only the other kids have cancer, too."

"You just won't be the only bald ones," Riley quips.

I give him a mock glare and rub my head. "We're not bald anymore, Riley," I say. "My hair's longer than yours, now."

"When do we leave?" Mackenzie asks excitedly. "Where is it? For how long?"

"It's east of Thibodaux; about twenty minutes away. It's for the first two weeks of August."

Mackenzie and I do an impromptu dance around the dining room table. "Summer camp, here we come!" she laughs.

Princess suddenly races into the room and runs between our legs. Mackenzie trips over her and falls into me, causing us both to collapse on the floor in a heap. Princess yelps and retreats under the table.

"Settle down, girls," Mom says, exasperated. "Come finish your dinner! And someone get that dog out of here!" Mamie comes and shoes the dog out while Mackenzie and I sit back down at the table. But the mood remains festive.

After supper, Mackenzie and I retreat to our room to talk about summer camp.

"I've never been away for two whole weeks," Mackenzie states, flopping back on her bed.

"At least we'll be together," I add, stroking Princess' back absently. "Do you think we'll get to do cool stuff, like canoeing and playing sand volleyball?"

"Probably," Mackenzie answers. "Do you think they'll be any cute guys there?"

I just roll my eyes at her.

Eventually we get ready for bed and settle down to sleep. Princess relaxes in her pink bed in the corner of the room. As I fall asleep, I send a quick 'thank you' up to God for summer camp.

The next morning, I get another phone call from Mrs. Turner.

"Hello, Taylor, thanks *so* much for taking care of Princess! We are home from the hospital now, and were wondering if you would mind bringing Princess over? I just *can't* leave my baby girl alone when she's hurt like this."

I assure Mrs. Turner that we can deliver the dog, and go inform Mom of our new morning plans.

"We can stop in Thibodaux and get Evangeline a card and maybe a balloon," Mom suggests. "That would be a thoughtful thing to do."

Normally I would have balked at getting Evangeline a gift, but I know how it is to be laid up, and how good it feels to know that other people are thinking of you.

I run out to the stables, where Mackenzie is grooming Oakley.

"We're leaving at ten o'clock," I tell her. "We need to take Princess back to the Turner's and get a get-well present for Evangeline." Surprisingly, my sister doesn't complain about getting Evangeline a gift, either.

"As long as we don't have to pay for it," is her response.

Half an hour later, we pile into the Camaro with Mom and head for Thibodaux. The city is bustling this morning, and it takes longer than normal to reach Walmart. If Evangeline knew she was getting a gift from Walmart, she would probably end up back in the hospital with a blown artery or something, but we can't afford three hundred dollar gifts all the time.

Mom picks up a few groceries while Mackenzie and I browse the store's selection of giant balloons.

"Looks like it's either 'Happy birthday' or a giant monkey face," I comment dryly as we look up at the balloons. "Does nobody think to stock 'Get well soon' balloons?"

Mackenzie stares up at the balloons thoughtfully. "What if we just got her flowers or something?" she suggests. "Or that shiny pink one? We could always write a message on it for her."

"Let's go with flowers," I agree hastily. "I sure don't want to be around when that balloon pops and Princess decides to eat it."

Mackenzie laughs. "You don't want to send that dog to the vet for an emergency more than once."

"It was an *accident*!!" I protest. I'm never going to live down the chocolate cake episode, at least not with my sister.

We find a decent bouquet of spring flowers and a card with a Yorkie on the front and go look for Mom. She waves at us from the checkout and we hurry over.

Mom looks at the card for a moment. "You realize we don't have any pens in the car, right? How are you two going to sign it?"

"Oh, we were just going to give it to her blank," Mackenzie replies with a mischievous grin. "Then she can write whatever she wants in it and pretend it was us who said it."

Mom rolls her eyes and asks the cashier if there is a pen we can borrow. The cashier, a nice old lady with purple hair, smiles kindly, hands us a pen with the store's logo on it, and tells us to keep it. Free advertising, I guess.

On the way to the Turner's, Mackenzie and I debate long and hard about what to put in the card.

"We can't say, 'to our dear friend', because she's not really a friend," Mackenzie says.

"Neither can we say, 'Dear enemy'," I retort. "No matter how hard I try to love her, most days, that's what she feels like."

"But if all we say is, 'To Evangeline', it sounds like our mom *made* us give her a card," Mackenzie responds.

"Which is kind of what actually happened," I point out.

Up front in the driver's seat, Mom sighs loudly. "I know you two don't get along with Evangeline, but for crying out loud, *writing a card isn't that difficult!!*"

That shuts us both up. Mom rarely raises her voice at any of us kids, so she is clearly getting very annoyed.

Mackenzie grabs the pen and quickly writes,

'Evangeline,

We hope you feel better soon and heal quickly,

Your friends, Mackenzie and Taylor.'

"There," she says, putting the card in the envelope and setting it with the flowers on the seat between us. "All we said is that we're *Evangeline's* friends, and Mrs. Turner herself said we are."

Mom just rolls her eyes at us.

We turn down the Turner's long, winding lane. In the passenger seat up front, Princess begins enthusiastically thumping her tail against the walls of her carrier. A minute later, we pull up in front of the Turner's elegant mansion and grind to a halt. Mackenzie and I scramble out of the backseat with the flowers and card and race up to the front porch, leaving Mom to lug the dog and her accessories up the steps.

Mackenzie uses the brass knocker to announce our arrival, and soon the Turner's butler opens the door. Mrs. Turner comes rushing up behind him.

"Oh, I'll let these guests in, Phil. Come in, come in!" Mrs. Turner gushes. She holds her arms out for the dog, and Mom gratefully releases a whining Princess into her custody.

"Phil, take the gear," Mrs. Turner announces briskly. "You know where it belongs."

Phil obligingly takes the mountain of possessions out of Mom's grasp, and disappears with it.

"Now, you *must* stay for tea, Mrs. Everett. And Evangeline is upstairs resting in her room if you girls would like to see her. Oh, you brought her flowers? How sweet! I'll send the maid up with a vase later."

We gratefully take our cue to disappear upstairs. Mackenzie leads the way up the winding oak stairs up to the top floor. Evangeline's room is directly on the right. The door is open, and I can see Evangeline lying on her back on the bed, her left foot propped up on a pillow. We tiptoe in hesitantly.

Evangeline turns her head to us as we enter and smiles.

"Hi guys," she says softly. She pulls herself up a little.

"Hey, Evangeline. Uh-we brought you some flowers, and, um, brought Princess back," I say.

Evangeline's eyes light up when I mention her dog.

"How was she?" she asks.

"Oh, you know...she only barfed on the carpet once. But I guess maybe that's because we fed her a cupcake. She was just looking at me with these big pleading eyes, so I just *had* to give her one, you know?"Mackenzie says nonchalantly. Evangeline's eyes get bigger.

I elbow my sister in the ribs. "She's kidding," I assure Evangeline. "Princess got exactly 4 oz. of Chicken and Veggie Stew."

Evangeline relaxes a little. "Well, thanks for keeping her, guys. I knew I could trust her with you two, because you have experience with animals."

Not too long ago, our 'experience with animals' would have been another reason for Evangeline to look down on us country bumpkins, but it seems that things have changed.

"How did you break your leg, anyway?" I ask curiously.

Evangeline looks a little embarrassed.

"Well, remember how on the last day of school, Mackenzie said you guys were looking forward to climbing on your roof again to go stargazing? Well, I tried it, but the night I picked was really cloudy, and then I dropped my flashlight halfway up to the peak, and there was no moon that night, so when I was trying to get down, I kind of slipped and fell." Her words come out in a rush.

"Uh, definitely check the weather next time," Mackenzie tells her. "Dad only lets us go up there on nights when it's clear and he makes us wear head lamps to get up. Plus, he makes us use a ladder to get up."

"Well, I couldn't use a ladder, or Mom would get suspicious for sure. I just climbed out the bathroom window onto the balcony roof, and got up that way. And I don't think there will be a 'next time'," Evangeline says sadly. "Mom was furious. She said I have no business on the roof. If God wanted me to go that high, he would have given me wings."

I bite my lips to keep in a giggle, but the laughter makes its way out of me with a weird snorting noise. I turn away from Evangeline and try to contain myself.

What happens next surprises me. I hear Evangeline giggle, and soon the three of us have dissolved into laughter. Mackenzie is practically rolling around on the floor, and I'm trying to figure why we're all acting like this when nothing is really *that* funny. Evangeline gets control of herself first, but she sets us off again by saying, " I guess I should have told my mom that birds go on the ground, too, so maybe us 'groundlings' *are* meant to go up high. But I guess that wouldn't have been very respectful."

Finally, I wipe away the tears from my eyes and rescue the flowers and card from where Mackenzie dropped them on the floor. The one flower is mangled, its head dangling awkwardly from the stem.

"Here are the flowers we brought you," I say, handing them to Evangeline. "Sorry, the one got a little wrecked."

She responds by plucking off the flower head and putting it in her hair, before tossing the stem at Mackenzie, who is still lying on the floor, catching her breath.

"We almost got you a balloon, but the only ones were either Birthday ones, or lame, or had faces on them," Mackenzie gasps, sitting upright. The flower stem falls from its resting place on her shoulder.

"It's good you didn't. You probably would've popped it by now," Evangeline giggles. "Although it would have been fun to have a Holstein dog balloon..."

Mackenzie bark-moos at Evangeline just as the maid comes in the door behind us. The maid gives Mackenzie an odd look, probably trying to decide if she is okay, and hands a vase to Evangeline before hurriedly retreating.

"At least it wasn't my mom who came in," Evangeline laughs.

Before we know it, the maid fetches me and Mackenzie to go home. As I quickly sign Evangeline's cast, I wonder what happened between us. We used to just tolerate her, and now it looks like we might actually be friends! It's like the pastor at church *was* right all along, and it *is* possible to turn enemies into friends, with God's help. I'm starting to feel a little ashamed at the way I always treated the aristocrats.

I think about this strange thing all the way home.

IV

August

"Let us dance in the sun, wearing wild flowers in our hair...."
Susan Polis Schutz

12

Chapter 12

The sun shines brightly in the hot blue August sky. The lob lolly pines on either side of the narrow asphalt road stand straight and tall. Up ahead, a sign comes into view.

The words "Hope Summer Camp" are splashed in blue across a yellow background. I squeeze Mackenzie's hand. For the next two weeks, this will be our home-away-from-home.

Mom turns the SUV down a wide dirt lane. We crest a small hill. Down in the valley the camp is spread out before us on the shores of a small lake.

I can see a large log building surrounded by giant oaks. A pathway leads down to a cluster of cabins by the water. A large dock juts out from the left. A few fishing boats are moored there, and a rack of kayaks sits up against a small shack. There's a barn over in a clearing across from the log house. I can see horses, a soccer field, and mini golf down by a creek. A baseball diamond is at the far end of the valley.

We drive through a tunnel of trees and arrive at the large log building. Signs hang over various doors, leading to the Main Office, Chapel, Cafeteria, Lounge, or Restrooms.

We lug our suitcases into the office. A lady with purple lipstick and a name tag reading "Catherine" taps away at a computer behind the desk. Her brightly dyed hair is frizzed in a large puff around her head.

She glances up at us as we shuffle inside. An awkward silence follows.

"Mackenzie and Taylor Everett," Mom says finally.

She clicks around a little more, then sits back for the first time.

"You girls are in the 'Sparrow' Cabin. Your counselor is Madison Wells. Follow the path with the 'Cabins' sign and dump your stuff in the 'Sparrow' Cabin, then come back to the Chapel for orientation." Catherine takes a deep breath as though that little paragraph exhausted her, purses her purple lips and slumps into her chair to resume her clicking.

I shoot Mackenzie a sideways glance. She's biting her lip, trying not to laugh at Catherine.

We follow Mom down a trail covered with wood chips. The 'Sparrow' Cabin is the third of about a dozen, trim, log cabins. It sits directly across from the strip of sand bordering the lake.

Inside, the cabin consists of three rooms: a single bedroom, a bathroom, and a communal bunk room with four sets of bunk beds. Three of the bunks already have bags sitting on them. Mackenzie and I quickly bag the bunk in the back corner. "Top or bottom?" I ask my sister.

She scrunches her nose a little. "I'll take the bottom," she says finally. I shove my suitcase in the space between our bunk and the one in front of it, and toss my backpack up to the top. "So if the top bunk breaks, you'll be at the bottom of the pile," I tease her as she settles her stuff under the bed.

She gives me a look that could melt ice cream in the Arctic. Mom just shakes her head at me and chuckles.

We're just leaving the cabin when a short, slight girl with tiny pigtails enters. She seems to radiate energy. "Hi, guys," she says, practically bouncing into the room. "I'm Tasha." Then she laughs and points to her own head. "Hey, same hairstyles."

I grin at her and shake my head so my pigtails flop around.

"Team Pigtail!" Mackenzie shouts.

Tasha grins and jumps around. "So, what are your names? Are you guys twins? You look kind of alike. That's so cool if you are! Have you been here before? I have, and it's awesome! The best parts are the horses, the lake, and the sports, and the food is amazing! The cook has been here, like, since my dad was a little kid. There's a climbing wall that's like, fifty feet high, and some cool trails. Oh, and if you like fishing, this lake is awesome for that. Last summer I caught an eleven-inch speckled trout. The camp record is a thirteen pound trout!"

Tasha tosses her bags on a bunk and follows us out the door, never stopping for a breath. She chatters all the way to the chapel. I just listen and smile. I think I've made my first camp friend.

The chapel is in the west wing of the great log main building. A bright stage sits at the front of the room, and chairs are set in rows in front of it. Mom hugs us goodbye, and we go to find a seat. The chairs are split into sections. We quickly go to the row marked 'Sparrows', and sit down beside Tasha.

Our counselor, Maddy, is a tall blonde with long hair and a "Camp Hope" T-shirt. A portly man with jet black hair steps up to the microphone. "Welcome to Camp Hope," he begins, "I hope we will all have a safe and happy time here these next two weeks."

I zone out as he begins reading the list of rules and regulations. I really don't want to hear them, anyway. I look around the auditorium. It seems as though the girls' cabins are all birds, and the guys' cabins are all wood animal names.

Directly in front of me, a tall kid with a thin covering of blonde hair turns in his chair and smirks at me. I give him a deadly stare. The last thing I need is for some guy to be watching me.

Another kid over in the "Raccoon" Cabin row is sporting a purple mullet that is obviously not his own hair. All around the room, kids are decked out in bows, ball caps, colorful wigs, or no hair at all. It really is a camp for kids with cancer.

After orientation, the blonde kid in front of me turns around and sticks his hand out.

"I'm Kobe," he says, grinning.

"Taylor," I say, shaking it hesitantly. Beside me, Tasha is introducing everyone in the 'Sparrow' Cabin to each other.

"This is Casey," she says, pointing to a girl with short, red curls; "and this is Mila. And this Mackenzie, and Taylor, and Lily. And you two haven't been here before," she adds, pointing to a bald girl with a huge pink bow, and a girl with wild curls.

Maddy is smiling like a fool. "Oh, I'm so glad y'all are gettin' to know each other!" she says in a high, squeaky tone. I've already decided that I do *not* like her voice when I feel a tap on my shoulder. I spin around to face a slight Asian girl.

"Are you girls twins?" she asks, pointing between me and Mackenzie.

I nod my head.

"For better or for worse," adds Mackenzie. I give her a light punch on the arm.

Introductions over, we all spill out of the building into the late morning sunshine.

The first activity of the day is getting our water safety certificates so we can go swimming and canoeing on the lake. The Sparrows head back to our cabin and get ready for the water. A slim, tanned woman with streaky blonde hair in a blue swim set is standing down by the dock, a whistle around her neck.

"Hey all, I'm Meg, counselor for the Robins and your swim instructor," she says as we all gather around her. "Everyone will be required to take a lap out to that white and red rope in the lake and back to pass the swim test."

The rope is about twenty-five meters out on the lake. Mackenzie and I have been swimming since we were four, so I'm not intimidated by it at all. Meg motions for me to go first.

"Run and dive off the dock and swim out," she instructs.

I fly across the wooden slats and dive down into the clear water. The lake feels amazing; the temperature is perfect. I set out for the rope, settling into a steady pace. Sunlight makes the water droplets I churn up look like diamonds, and the air is warm. I reach the rope in record time and circle back.

I climb up the ladder onto the dock, shaking the water from my face. I grin and give the next girl in line a thumbs up.

"Feels good!" I tell her.

After swim lessons, the whole camp gathers for a big game of soccer. The rest of the day is filled with activities, and by supper, I'm totally worn out.

That night in the cabin, I find out that Tasha is as mischievous as she is talkative.

Maddy leaves for a counselor's meeting after making sure we were settling into our bunks. As soon as she is out the door, Tasha switches the light on. "Hey guys, who says we have a little fun?" she asks, eyes gleaming.

Mila, who had bunked with Tasha last year, nods enthusiastically.

Her brown curls bounce against her mocha face.

"Tasha plans the best escapades," she announces.

"Come on Tasha, it's only the first night," Lily complains. "Let's all settle in before we get into trouble."

Erin, the bald girl, and curly-haired Nisha look as curious as I feel.

"I'd be down to have a little excitement," Mackenzie says from below me.

"Alright, well, first things first," Tasha says, sitting cross legged on her bunk, "you know that little section of grass behind the baseball diamond that's almost surrounded in trees?"

I think back over the tour we had taken.

"Uh-huh..." Erin murmurs.

"Well," Tasha continues, "Every year, on the last night, all the... brave... people meet back in that little spot for a little party. But until then, there are other ways to keep camp exciting. Like last year, when we short-sheeted the camp director's bed, or let loose a raccoon in the 'Hedgehog' Cabin." she gives us a sly smile, "that's the cabin that was sitting in front of us in the chapel. They always get the best guys."

I stick my head over the rail and grin down at Mackenzie. This sounds like just our kind of stuff. We don't try anything that night, yet, but the fire is lit.

The "Sparrow girls" are going places.

13

Chapter 13

The drops of water sparkle in the sunlight as they skitter off our paddles. It's free time, and Mackenzie and I decided to take advantage of passing the swim test and boat course, and go kayaking.

Lake Bellevue stretches over four acres. Cottages hug the coastline farther out. The camp's main building is now just a speck at the other end of the water. I deftly turn left and skirt around a small island.

"Hey, let's go explore that river," Mackenzie says, pointing to a small waterway that snakes off from the lake.

I turn my kayak and follow Mackenzie. We enter the mouth of the river. Tall oaks and willows bend down over the water. The river is cool and dark. Up ahead, an old gentleman is seated on a chair on his dock, a fishing pole resting against his arm. We wave and paddle silently around him.

A stone bridge looms up ahead. A car rattles over it as we slow our kayaks underneath. I look up at the mass of stones arcing overhead.

"Cool place," Mackenzie comments.

"I wonder how old that bridge is," I wonder aloud.

"It sure is cool," answers a voice from the shadows. Two kayaks slide out from within the reeds just beyond the bridge. The blonde guy, Kobe, is sitting in a kayak beside a Hispanic boy.

"What are you guys doing here?" I ask, startled.

The Hispanic kid grins. "I had to take Kobe out here. I've been at camp five years in a row now, and he's never seen it," he says. "And in answer to your other question, this bridge was built over seventy years ago, in 1949. The middle had to be rebuilt back in 1998, but the original structure is still all there at the ends."

"You could be a history teacher," Kobe teases.

I introduce Kobe to Mackenzie, and the other guy says his name is Mateo. He lives in the area, and attends this camp every year. He's had leukemia twice- once when he was five, and then two years ago.

Kobe says it's his first, and probably his last summer at camp. His cancer is progressing too fast to treat, so he's trying to make the best of the last year of his life. When his friend, Mateo, invited him to camp, he just knew he had to take the chance.

We paddle slowly back to the camp, enjoying the bird calls and sunshine and the music of paddles dipping into the water. I think about Kobe, and how I can't imagine knowing you will probably die within a few months. When I had cancer, I knew I could die, but I was too sick to care much. Life was consumed with trying to get better. Kobe's life is just a waiting game.

By the time we get back to the dock, I am so tired. We've missed lunch, and most of the camp is out on the soccer field, playing Frisbee.

The cook makes us sit down in the kitchen and eat something. By now, Kobe is pale, and shaking with fatigue. Mateo looks at him worriedly.

"I know you want to spend the rest of your time making memories and stuff, but I think you outdid yourself this time, buddy," Mateo mutters.

After a bit of food, the camp nurse helps Mateo carry Kobe back to their cabin to rest. "Do you think he'll be alright?" Mackenzie asks worriedly.

"I hope so," I answer.

The Frisbee game is still going strong when Mackenzie and I reach the field, but I can only play half-heartedly. I don't see Mateo until suppertime. I catch his eye, and he flashes me a thumbs up. I hope that means that Kobe is recovering.

After supper, while the rest of the camp is gathered around a fire, my sister and I sneak off to Kobe's cabin with Mateo.

The girls aren't allowed in the boys' cabins, and vice versa, but this is an emergency.

The 'Hedgehog' Cabin is almost identical to the 'Sparrow' Cabin. On the bottom bunk in the back corner, a lump is lying down beneath the blankets. Kobe flashes us his familiar grin and waves weakly.

"How's it going?" I ask him. I try to sound natural, and not too worried. I know from experience that when you're sick, you don't want people pitying you. Sometimes, some people act almost like your cancer is contagious.

"Doing better. Just overdid the kayaking, I guess. With a good night's sleep, I'll be perky tomorrow," he replies.

A knock sounds on the door. "Quick, hide!" Mateo whispers. "It's the nurse! You two aren't supposed to be here!"

I duck into the counselor's bedroom and slide into the closet, Mackenzie right behind me. I shut the closet door almost all the way as the nurse enters the cabin.

"How's my patient, today?" she asks in a chirpy voice. I can hear her moving around, chattering all the while. She gives him food and medicine, and stays for a bit to talk.

I'm starting to get a little worried. I can see the counselor's alarm clock from the crack in the closet door.

"8:02. We should have lots of time," I think to myself.

Finally the nurse leaves. It's now 8:30. I'm Just about to open the closet door when another pair of footsteps enters the cabin.

"How's it going, Champ?" a deep voice asks.

Beside me, I hear Mackenzie gasp. It sounds like Kobe and Mateo's counselor.

And we are in his closet.

"I just need to grab a sweater, and then I'll leave you two alone if you're doing all right, " I hear him say.

My blood turns cold.

"Taylor, we've gotta get out of here!" Mackenzie whispers frantically.

"Here, use mine!" We hear Mateo offer quickly.

The counselor laughs loudly. "You're too small, buddy, but thanks for the offer."

Mackenzie clutches my arm hard enough to cut off the circulation as the footsteps move into the bedroom. There is no escape.

I watch as a few fingers grab the edge of the door, inches from my elbow.

Then he flings open the door... and screams.

14

Chapter 14

1849, August 9

Dear Diary,

Big Jim's wounds have healed into an ugly mass of scars. Massa say it hard to sell a slave with scars like that– everybody knows he's a runaway.

Tom still hasn't been caught. We're hoping and praying that he either made it to Canada or is getting close.

Ol' George says he heard in town that a girl about my age was found to be able to read. Her Massa whipped her so hard she couldn't stand it, and she died the next day. Momma says for me to take it as a warning to be extra careful. She don't know I have a writing book like this. I'm not sure if she would be more proud or disapproving. I think mostly she'd be scared, but I have these words inside, this story to tell, and I have to get it out.

The stench of fear hangs over the plantation like a cloud, and Prissy sure is taking advantage of it. She asks me to do the most ridiculous things because she knows that after Big Jim, we don't dare protest or roll our eyes about it.

If I ever get free, which isn't likely, I'm gonna make sure I never treat no

one like Prissy treats me.
  Nora Mae Washington

∞ ∞ ∞ ∞ ∞

Kobe is doing a lot better now, and Mackenzie and I didn't even get in too much trouble for being found in a boys' cabin. The director just said he 'understands' our worry and 'doesn't blame us." He did put us on dish washing duty for the next two evenings, though.

Camp is going so fast. So far Tasha hasn't been able to get a major prank together. We did put hot sauce in the soup one day, and put washable paint in our counselor's shampoo, but Mila says Tasha doesn't seem to have her act put together this year. But Tasha promises that we'll end the year off well. We've been throwing around epic prank ideas in the 'Sparrow' Cabin, and so far Nisha's idea is winning.

Our cabin has been elected to do a Bible skit on Sunday in chapel, along with the Hedgehog's, so on Friday evening, after Mackenzie and I finished our last dish washing duty, we headed to the chapel to root through costumes and plan our skit.

"Let's do 'Esther'!" Tasha suggests, perching a crown on her head. "Us girls can be Esther, Queen Vashti, and the princesses the king picked from. The guys can be the king, Mordecai, Haman, and some soldiers or something!"

Everyone jumps on that idea.

Mackenzie is elected to be Esther, and Mateo is Mordecai. Kobe is Haman, and a kid named Evan, with shockingly red hair, is the king. And I am Queen Vashti.

"Here's a rope we can use to 'hang' Haman!" Mateo yells enthusiastically from backstage.

Mackenzie drapes a silk shawl over my shoulders and bows. "There, Queen Vashti," she says solemnly.

"Hey, here are some beggar's clothes for Mordecai!" Evan calls from the depths of the costume chest. "And a dagger for Haman!"

All the girls sort through the box of gowns, shawls and tiaras.

"Mackenzie needs the best dress, because she's Esther," Tasha announces, pulling out a rich cobalt blue, flowing garment.

"And here's purple for the 'queen'," Mila says, tossing me a royal purple dress.

There are shields and swords for the royalty, and robes for Haman. In fact, the camp's costume collection seems to hold everything you could ever want or use in a play, right down to a ratty mouse costume and a very home-made looking giraffe head. We all slip on our costumes, and set to work acting out Haman's evil plot, Esther's courage, and the story of saving the Jews.

∞ ∞ ∞ ∞ ∞

The chapel is packed. I never realized how many kids are actually at the camp, until they're all staring at me, seated on my 'throne' on stage beside Evan.

"I am going to have a party, Queen Vashti, and I want you to come before everyone at the party after dessert so they can see you, because you are so beautiful."

Evan looks at me over the top of his very bushy, very fake black beard. It doesn't match his hair at all. I stand up and swirl my skirts around me.

"Am I just an ornament? A fancy object to look upon?" I practiced my high shrieks last night, and I think I pull off a pretty indignant sounding one onstage.

"Yes, that is exactly what I am asking of you, Oh Queen," Evan says, trying to sound annoyed.

"I refuse!" I scream.

"Throw her out!" Evan yells angrily, and two of the boys, daggers hanging at their sides, rush onto the stage and pull me off.

"I now call my right-hand servant to the throne," Evan says loudly, and a boy named Carter, dressed in a long black robe with a red sash, hurries on stage.

"Oh Samuel, I now beseech you to bring me all the fair virgins of the land that I may choose a new queen," Evan instructs. Carter bows and hurries off stage.

Backstage, the girls are dressed in royal clothes, waiting for their turn to go on stage. One of them helps me pull the curtain closed, and Haman and Mordecai prepare to go on stage. Mateo found a wooden fence that we put on stage to be the 'gate' where Mordecai sits, and Mateo makes himself comfortable against it. A few other boys, dressed in ill fitting clothes and ratty beards, join him. I pull back the curtain, again.

Kobe, aka Haman, swaggers across the stage. A few old men lounge by the city gate. They all bow to him, except for the most poorly dressed of them all.

Haman turns and gives the man the evil eye.

"Who are you?" he demands.

"Mordecai the Jew," answers Mateo.

"Why do you not bow?"

"I bow only to God," is the answer.

"You will pay for this."

The scene changes back to the king on his throne. I watch from backstage as the rest of the girls parade in front of him. Evan points his broom handle, or golden scepter, at Mackenzie.

"I believe you are the fairest of them all. What is your name, oh beautiful one?"

The audience thinks it's hilarious that Evan calls Mackenzie beautiful, and I have a feeling they might both get teased a little after this.

"I am Esther," Mackenzie answers.

The king stands and crowns Esther as the new queen. The other girls all pretend to look disappointed, and run off the stage.

The next scene features Haman's devious plan. Because of his secret grudge against Mordecai, he comes to the king and requests that all the

Jews be killed. The king agrees, not knowing that his own queen is a Jew.

Mackenzie goes back on stage, and tries to overthrow the nasty plot. After throwing two banquets for the king, and not gaining the courage to speak up, she finally approaches the king uninvited– a royal faux pa punishable by death– and ultimately saves the Jewish race.

In the last and final scene, Mateo throws the rope around Kobe's neck and pretends to hang Haman. The rest of the campers cheer loudly.

15

Chapter 15

It's Wednesday; only three days left of camp. And by now, I'm kind of ready to go back home. I just want to do one epic prank before we leave.

When we get to our cabin that night, Tasha gathers us in a circle in the middle of the bunk room floor.

"I have everything planned out," she explains in low tones. "This is going to be a prank like Hope Camp has never seen before." Quickly she outlines the details. We all think it's a great plan. It looks like I'll get the epic prank I've been wanting.

"We don't leave until Saturday noon, so people will have enough time to recover. On Friday night... we strike."

oo oo oo oo oo

I lie down in my bunk, listening carefully for the quiet snores of our counselor. Tasha gets up silently and creeps to the closed door of the counselor's bedroom. She presses an ear to the door. She listens for a moment, then flashes us a thumbs up. Each member of the 'Sparrow' Cabin creeps softly out the door.

It is Friday night. We had reviewed our stations the night before, and we all skitter off into the shadows to perform our tasks. Tasha and Casey are headed to the 'Hedgehog' Cabin, while Mila and Nisha go to the 'Opossum' Cabin. Lily and Erin have the 'Robins'.

Mackenzie and I head down to the docks after making a detour to the dumpsters. I'm panting by the time we reach the canoes with our heavy load. Mackenzie grins at me as she plops a garbage bag into a canoe. I lift up the tarp and put mine in the other end. Soon the canoe is filled with lumpy shapes, and we secure the tarp over it securely.

"Wait, what if the canoe floats to the middle of the lake? We want it close enough that people will try to rescue it," Mackenzie says suddenly.

"Weren't you listening to Tasha? We get to wade out, drop the anchors, and wade back in," I reply.

Mackenzie groans.

"But first, let's fill the other canoe," I say.

We head back to the dumpster. Soon the two canoes, filled with mysterious lumps, float side by side at the dock.

I dip a toe in the water and grimace. Swimming at eleven o'clock at night in my pajamas is not my favorite thing to do.

"What are we gonna do?" Mackenzie whispers. "I sure don't want to have to take care of my wet pajamas and keep the counselor from seeing them."

"There are some random clothes on a shelf in the boathouse," I whisper back. "I saw them when I was putting back my life jacket the other day."

Mackenzie grabs my hand. "Come on! Oh, and there are towels in the boating hut, too, I think." We sneak over to the side door of the boat hut and try turning the knob. It's unlocked. I make my way through the dark hut, tripping over a life ring and knocking down a paddle in the process.

"Shhhh," Mackenzie hisses.

"I'm trying!" Finally I reach the shelf at the back and reach up for a shadowy pile. A bunch of clothes topple down onto my head."

"Found them!" I say triumphantly.

We hold the clothes up to the window, trying to see what there is in the faint moonlight streaming in. Mackenzie plucks a massive striped tank top off the pile and holds it up.

"Guess I'll wear this," she giggles. I throw her some shorts and find some clothes for myself.

"Okay, let's go!" I whisper nervously.

Mackenzie just grins and leads the way out to the lake. As we head out into the moonlight and really glimpse each other, we burst into fits of giggles. My pair of shorts are extra large boy's swim trunks, and I have them cinched as tight as possible at the waist, but the legs still balloon down past my knees. My shirt is neon yellow and tight, while Mackenzie's tank top reaches halfway to her knees, completely covering the short black shorts she found. We laugh all the way down to the water's edge.

We tiptoe cautiously in. Without the sun shining down, the water is freezing cold. A slight breeze blows over my shoulders as I stand knee-deep in the water, and I begin to shiver.

Mackenzie and I pull the canoes out until we're chin deep in the lake. I grin at her through chattering teeth as we drop the anchors and head back to the dock. By now, my legs feel numb.

"This is... kinda fun," I admit.

We pull ourselves up on the dock and run to the boathouse.

I struggle to move in the now wet, massive shorts. They wrap around my legs and I almost trip across the threshold into the boathouse.

"Careful," Mackenzie giggles.

We quickly finish changing and hang our towels and wet clothes over the rack in the boat hut, then scamper outside.

The others are waiting for us under the tree behind our cabin.

"It went perfectly!" Tasha whispers, eyes gleaming. "Everyone has already packed their bags, so it was simple to steal them. And no one woke up on us!"

Nisha grins under her mop of wild curls. "I can't wait to see their faces tomorrow morning when they think their bags are out on the lake in the canoes!"

"And then they'll get themselves all wet to rescue canoes full of garbage!" Milo whispers excitedly.

"And all the time, their bags are just hiding in the trees around the soccer field!" Mackenzie finishes.

"Did you two remember to put the notes in the canoes? These people will need a little help finding their stuff," Tasha turns to Mackenzie and me.

I nod. "Yup. It says, 'You got wet for nothing. Go climb a tree!" I grin. I personally came up with that riddle.

We creep back to our cabin through the darkness, and hide our own bags under the beds so we aren't picked out as the culprits immediately. In the counselor's room, Maddy is still snoring.

I lie down in my bed, still giddy with excitement and adrenaline. I can't wait for tomorrow.

When we get up the next morning, a bunch of kids are already gathering on the beach. "Our stuff!" Evan wails, "It's all out in the lake!"

We melt into the crowd, pretending to be as surprised as everyone else.

I bite back a smile as Mateo and a kid from the 'Opossum' Cabin head out to the canoes.

"It's cold!" Mateo yells as he gets in up to his waist.

Almost the whole camp, including the counselors, have gathered on the beach by the time Mateo and the other guy reach the canoes.

Tasha gives me a nudge as the boys struggle to lift the anchors in water up to their chins.

The camp director comes out just as Mateo and the other guy reach the dock with the still covered canoes. Mateo ties both canoes to the dock, and the members of the cabins whose bags have been taken swarm around him as he pulls back the tarp.

Cries of dismay go up in the crowd as everyone sees what is actually beneath the tarps. Each canoe holds four big, black garbage bags. A stench is already wafting from them in the early morning heat.

"Wait!" Mateo yells, "There's a note!" He holds up his hand and everyone quiets down.

"You got wet for nothing. Go climb a tree," He reads.

"They're in a tree!" Kobe yells from the dock. "Everyone, go search the trees!"

All the campers and counselors spread out over the camp. Mackenzie and I go with Mateo and Kobe. "I can't believe someone stole our bags without us waking up," Kobe says, shaking his head.

"Hey, at least you didn't get wet for nothing," Mateo retorts. He sounds a little mad.

"I wonder who did this," Mackenzie says innocently.

Kobe shakes his head. "Who knows."

We're peering up into trees near the mini golf course when a shout goes up from the soccer field. Everyone rushes over there.

Tasha and the rest of the girls had done a good job. Piles of bags are suspended in half a dozen trees, just out of reach from the ground. The director comes over as Kobe gets ready to scale a tree.

"No one climbs the trees," he instructs. "Safety first. I will go get a ladder and get them down. I don't know who did this," he says, stern eyes sweeping the crowd, "but it was a good prank," he finishes with a smile.

My shoulders slump a little in relief. I sure wouldn't want to get in hot water on the last day. The director soon comes back with a ladder and a knife. One by one, the bags come thumping down from the trees as he cuts the ropes. Soon all the kids have their bags back. I just hope no one had any fragile objects along. Mackenzie grins at me as Mateo goes grumbling back to his cabin to change out of his wet clothes.

It was a good prank, indeed. Maybe Tasha hasn't lost her touch, after all.

V

September

I used to love September, but now it just rhymes with remember.
–Dominic Riccitello

16

Chapter 16

"Taylor, I don't feel good," Mackenzie says.

It's the second week of school, and we're just getting back into the routine. We're still sunburned from camp, but most of the high has faded.

"Maybe you're just tired," I say. I look up from where I'm picking out my outfit for the day. My sister looks pale against the blue covers.

"Okay, you look more than tired. What's wrong?" I ask.

She smiles thinly. "I must be coming down with a flu. And can you get me another blanket? I'm freezing."

I grab a thick, fuzzy blanket from the top shelf of our closet, and wrap it around Mackenzie. She's shaking with chills.

"I'll go get Mom," I say. Worry is starting to creep around inside.

I race downstairs. Mom is eating a pastry in the kitchen, her hair still falling loose about her shoulders.

"Mom, Mackenzie thinks she has the flu," I pant.

Mom gets up and hurries upstairs. I follow her. Mom turns to me just outside the door. "Get dressed, Taylor. You might as well go to school," she says.

"But Mom," I protest.

"There is no use sitting around here worrying, honey," she says softly. I sigh and nod.

"I'm sure it's just a routine flu," Mom encourages. That does little to thaw the icy ball of worry in the pit of my stomach. This feels so familiar.

School does not go well that day. In Math, we have a pop quiz and I can't remember half the answers, even though it's all Review. In English, I daydream and get scolded, and in History, when it's my turn at the map and Miss Hildebrandt asks me to point to China, I put my finger on Argentina, which is in a totally different continent.

I can't help but remember the last time my sister and I came down with a 'flu.' Only that flu didn't go away, and it ended up being leukemia.

"But if it is leukemia, surely I would have it, too," I reason. "Mackenzie and I usually get sick together." I can't, and won't, imagine my twin sister having to go through cancer again by herself. If Mackenzie has to suffer, so do I.

That night, I climb into Mackenzie's bed with her. Her teeth are chattering while her skin burns. Dark circles of fatigue are under her eyes, even though she's slept all day.

She clutches my hand under the sheets and whispers, "Taylor, I think it's coming back."

"No!" I protest, "it's just the flu! You'll get over this, Mackenzie!"

She shakes her head. "This feels exactly like last time: the fever, the chills, the fatigue..."

"Mom's taking us to the hospital for our September check-up tomorrow," I argue, "and August's came back clear. So will September's! You'll be fine, Mackenzie!"

Her eyes fill with tears and she squeezes my hand. "I hope so," she pauses. "I've been feeling a little weak for the past two weeks. I thought it was just starting school, but..."

"And you didn't tell me?" I whisper fiercely.

"I didn't want to worry you, Taylor, and I didn't think anything of it. It wasn't bad; I just felt tired a lot," she explains. She stares up at the ceiling for a while. Finally she whispers, "Taylor, I'm scared."

So am I.

∞ ∞ ∞ ∞ ∞

The New Orleans Children's Hospital looks the same as last time, yet different.

Nurse Emily leads us to a room in the Oncology department. I look in the open doorway to the 'chemo room'. Five dentist-like chairs are spread out across the floor, some occupied. IV stands are by each chair, ready to drip cancer-killing chemicals into a child's veins. Last autumn that had been me. This autumn, it might be Mackenzie- for the second time.

I wipe my sweaty palm on my pink hospital gown as Mackenzie and I are led to separate rooms. Besides our usual blood tests, Dr. Lindsey wants to do a bone marrow exam. I am not looking forward to having a needle shoved into my lower back to suck out some of my bone marrow.

Mackenzie looks paler than she did yesterday. I can tell Dr. Lindsey is worried. Well, so am I.

I know there is just as much of a chance that my cancer could be coming back, too, but right now, I'm not even worried about that. I just want Mackenzie to be clear again.

Nurse Emily checks my heart rate and blood pressure, and then I curl up on the exam table with my knees drawn up to my chest. I silently pray that Mackenzie will be okay.

Dr. Lindsay comes in and marks the area for the aspiration and biopsy. I've had an aspiration done before- taking the fluid out of bone marrow- but never a biopsy- taking a solid sample from your bone marrow. But the aspiration is supposed to be more painful than the biopsy, so I'm not too nervous about that one.

I feel something cold on my back, as the doctor cleans the area with antiseptic. She covers me with a drape, and then I feel Nurse Emily's arms tighten around me. She has to hold me absolutely still for the aspiration. Dr. Lindsey numbs the area and makes a small incision, before she sticks a hollow needle into my back.

I squeeze my eyes shut against the sharp pain that follows as the needle enters my bone, and I try to focus on something else.

The nurses always say to imagine yourself in a 'happy place' during the aspirations. I focus on riding Stormy through the woods. The trees nod at me in the breeze, and the grass waves in the clearing. And there, lying in the grass, is a rusty pair of shackles....

"Oh, why did I think about that?" I think as I abruptly return to the blue walls of the hospital room.

"And, done," Dr. Lindsey says, withdrawing the needle. She has collected a few vials of clear liquid from my bones. I sigh and relax a little, but Nurse Emily keeps holding me down.

"Now for the biopsy..." Dr. Lindsay announces. She sticks an even bigger needle into my back, to draw out the solid sample of marrow, but this one doesn't hurt as bad. Finally, she withdraws it and slaps a piece of gauze over the incision to help stop the bleeding. Nurse Emily helps me roll onto my back to keep pressure on the gauze.

"Dr. Trent is doing the exam on your sister right now. We just need to get some blood tests, and then we're done," Dr. Lindsey says cheerfully. "I'll be back in about fifteen minutes to collect the blood and check on the incision.

I lay back and stare at the white ceiling, trying not to think about what my sister is going through. The procedures are painful enough without already feeling like you've been hit by a cement truck.

"Please, God, please let Mackenzie be alright," I pray over and over.

After what seems like hours, Dr. Lindsey comes in and swabs my arm, before drawing up several vials of blood from my veins. I watch as the red liquid flows gets sucked out of my arm into the syringe. That blood is going to be one of two things– good, healthy blood, or an unhealthy indicator of something gone wrong in my body.

17

Chapter 17

A few nights after our trip to New Orleans, Mackenzie's nose begins to bleed. I sit by her bedside, holding her hand as Mackenzie hunches over a basin, shivering. Dad pinches the base of her nose in an attempt to staunch the bleeding. Mackenzie has still not shaken off her flu.

Downstairs, the phone rings. Everyone ignores it.

Riley sits down on the other side of Mackenzie's bed, stroking her forehead. We 're still waiting on the test results, but in my heart, I know.

Mackenzie is relapsing.

Mamie comes in the door just then, Mom's cell phone in hand.

"It's Dr. Lindsey," she whispers. Mom grabs it and holds it to her ear. Her face grows pale as she listens. Mackenzie's nose finally stops dripping crimson as Mom gets off the phone.

"Dr. Lindsey wants us to come to the hospital immediately. The test results are in," she says numbly. That can only mean one thing: the news isn't good.

Mamie offers to clean up the mess as Dad carefully carries Mackenzie to the car. I pray hard that her nose doesn't start bleeding again.

Dad drives to the hospital with the accelerator to the floor.

Dr. Lindsey meets us at the door of the hospital. She leads us up to an exam room in the Oncology department. She takes a seat on a hard plastic chair and shuffles her papers. "You've probably already figured this out based on Mackenzie's health lately, but the bone marrow tests show increased levels of irregular blood cells," she says, then pauses. "Mackenzie is relapsing."

I already knew it deep down inside, but hearing the words spoken out loud stuns me to the core.

"What about my tests?" I ask frantically. If Mackenzie has cancer, I have to have it, too. She *can't* go through it alone. If anyone has to suffer, it should be me.

"Taylor, your tests came back totally fine. You're still in remission," Dr. Lindsay says, giving me a small smile.

"So what's the next step?" Dad asks quietly.

Dr. Lindsey nods. "At this point, our best bet is a bone marrow transplant. We would need to start chemo again first, to kill all the cancerous bone marrow, and then suppress her immune system before giving her the transplant." She clears her throat. "We've already done a biopsy on Mom, Dad, and Riley. Obviously Taylor, as her identical twin, would be a perfect match, but although she's still in remission, it's obviously not possible since she just had cancer. Riley is our best match."

"She can have all the bone marrow she needs," Riley says quickly.

Dr. Lindsey smiles at him. "First we need to restart chemo. Mackenzie will be given high doses of chemo for the next four weeks, which will effectively destroy all the cells, both harmful and good, before going on immunosuppressant drugs. While on the immune suppressants, Mackenzie will be kept in a sterilized room. With her immune system suppressed and her good cells destroyed in the bone marrow, even a common cold can be deadly," the doctor explained. "After that, Riley's bone marrow will be intravenously given, much like a blood transfusion.

Mackenzie will be kept in a sterile room for anywhere from a week to a month, depending how long it takes for her body to recover. Any infections, or if her body rejects the bone marrow, will, of course, prolong the process."

The room falls silent. Here I was, still in remission, while my sister's immune system would be practically killed so she could–maybe– get cured.

"How dangerous is it?" Dad finally asks.

"With the transplant, Mackenzie has a fifty-fifty rate of survival. Without it she's down to about twenty per cent. Dr. Hobson, our bone marrow transplant specialist, will be able to give you more details."

"Well," Mackenzie says weakly from her chair, "since I want to live, let's do this."

◯◯ ◯◯ ◯◯ ◯◯ ◯◯

Dr. Hobson meets with us that afternoon and explains the transplant to us a little better.

He tells us that, "in Mackenzie's case, an *allogenic* transplant is best, where stem cells are donated from another person; in this case, it's Riley. Riley will undergo physical exams to make sure he is healthy and ready to donate. Then, his bone marrow will be collected from his hip area. He will be given a local anesthesia and a small incision will be made. A doctor will take some bone marrow fluid and collect it to give to Mackenzie. Meanwhile, Mackenzie will be doing chemotherapy to kill all the diseased cells and essentially 'empty' her bone marrow so there is room for the new, healthy cells from Riley. If everything goes well, the cells from Riley will sit happily in her bone marrow, and produce good blood cells. During the transplant time, Mackenzie will be kept in a sterile environment to help prevent diseases while her immune system is vulnerable, and until the stem cells start working to produce healthy blood cells. She will also take immunosuppressants to help prevent graft-vs-host disease, a condition where the new cells attack the host's organs. It typically takes 15-30 days for the new stem cells to start producing blood cells."

Everyone's head is swarming with all the new information. But we're ready. Because, like Mackenzie said, she wants to live, and we want her to live. She *has* to live, because I don't know if I can live without her.

VI

October

Anyone who thinks fallen leaves are dead has never watched
them dancing on a windy day.
−Shira Tamir

18

Chapter 18

Chemo starts almost immediately. If our side effects from before were bad, this is sheer torture. Mackenzie has developed sores in her mouth. She is constantly nauseous. The chemo doses are intense.

I haven't been back to school since the fateful diagnosis. So much for finally being in school for a whole year. As Mackenzie's chemo effectively destroys her bone marrow cells, she gets admitted to the hospital, and there is no way I'm going back to school alone while she is lying in a hospital bed. Her short hair all falls out again. I tie it up in a ribbon and hang it from the cork board in our room, for when Mackenzie comes home.

It doesn't seem fair. Why am I the healthy one, while Mackenzie slowly wastes away? Twins are supposed to do everything together.

Mackenzie's last week of chemo is scheduled for October 12. Two weeks after that, she will receive her bone marrow transplant. While Mackenzie sits in one of the dentist chairs, getting poisoned, and Riley undergoes dozens of tests, I wander the halls of the Oncology department.

"Why, God?" I scream in my head, "Why does this have to happen? I prayed, didn't I? I prayed that Mackenzie would be okay, but she's not. I thought you were supposed to heal people!"

Someone puts an arm around my shoulders and leads me to a nearby chair. I look up at my brother. I don't realize I am crying until Riley wipes my face with his shirt sleeve. He must be done all of his tests for today.

"Why did God let this happen?" I ask him desperately.

Riley shakes his head. "I don't know, baby, but it isn't His fault. God doesn't make the bad things happen. He's there for us through them, though."

"But I prayed, Riley," I cry onto his shoulder. "I thought God is supposed to answer prayers."

Riley sighs. "He does answer them. But every time I get torn up about it all to the point where I can barely cope, I just remind myself that if it doesn't work out, Mackenzie will be happier up in Heaven, dancing with the angels. And that would be the best thing that could ever happen to her."

I want to protest, to scream at him for even thinking that Mackenzie might die. It might be nicer for her, but what about those of us still on Earth? But I know he's right.

After a bit, Riley turns to me again. "Mackenzie's in the chemo room. She was asking if you could read from some diary or something."

I jump up and grab my backpack from the family room. The diary has been neglected during the past few weeks, but maybe it will help me and Mackenzie to keep our minds off of what is happening, at least for a little bit. Maybe Nora Mae Washington's story at least will end happily.

ᴑᴑ ᴑᴑ ᴑᴑ ᴑᴑ ᴑᴑ

1849, September 19
Dear Diary,

Today we had a close call at church in the clearing. Massa Andrews' foreman rode out in the woods, right near where we were. One of the lookouts warned us in time, and we were able to all sneak back to our huts.

Prissy is worse than ever. One of her friends is having a party, so she's constantly nagging me to try new hairstyles or polish her jewelry.

Big Jim got sold to a plantation in Mississippi. I pray every night that he's okay.

We still haven't heard nothing 'bout Tom. I'm going to think positive, though, and say that 'No news is good news.' (I heard Massa Andrews say that about a deal he made with someone the other day, and I like the ring of it, even if it did come from Massa.)

With all that's happened at the plantation recently, Papa keeps reminding us that we have to forgive our enemies, no matter how hard it is. So I'm trying to pray every night that God would help me to love and forgive the Andrews, even just a little bit. It's the hardest thing ever; it's even harder than watching Big Jim get whipped.

Nora Mae Washington

19

Chapter 19

The pale form beneath the white hospital sheet is just a shadow of the girl who used to be.

I sit beside Mackenzie, decked out in a gown, mask, gloves, and shoe covers. The room smells strongly of disinfectants. It's been scrubbed down thoroughly to kill every last germ and virus.

The monitors beep steadily. Mackenzie had started her immune suppressants yesterday. Riley is getting his bone marrow 'harvested' this afternoon. Mackenzie told me she was already sick of watching TV and reading, about the only two things to do in this room.

"Can you read me the rest of the diary?" she asks.

I sigh. "Nurse Emily said 'no'. The book isn't sterile."

Mackenzie groans weakly. "Sterile, sterile, sterile, that's the only word I hear anymore."

Nurse Emily comes in just then, and kicks me out so she can do a checkup on Mackenzie. I promise her I will finish the diary and tell her about it.

She just gets sicker over the next few days. Her legs swell up with the fluid. She gets put on a feeding tube because she can't keep anything down. And then one day, she's finally ready. A sample of her bone marrow shows that it's clean. My twin sister is virtually defenseless. It is an incredibly dangerous state to be in, yet it just might save her life.

∞ ∞ ∞ ∞ ∞

I flip idly through a magazine in the waiting room. I can't concentrate. Today is the day. Riley's bone marrow will be taken from storage in the freezer and dripped into Mackenzie's veins over the next five hours. Then she will stay in isolation while the doctors make sure her body accepts the new marrow, and the marrow doesn't fight her body.

Finally I pick up the diary. I promised my sister that I would read it, and tell her the parts she misses.

"I can fill her in on the ending when she goes into recovery," I tell myself. Recovery. Now *that's* a good word.

∞ ∞ ∞ ∞ ∞

1849, October 9

Dear Diary,

We just finished our church service in the woods. Massa Andrews has been real uptight, lately. He whips us for the slightest thing.

*I think Tom **must** have made it to Canada, because we haven't heard word of his arrest. I thank God for that every night.*

The clearing is so peaceful right now. People are all gathered around, talking. Sundays are good for the soul. Papa spoke on forgiveness today. He told us a story about a slave who was beat to death, and his last words to his massa were, 'I forgive you'. I don't know if I have that deep of a forgiveness to Massa Andrews or Prissy. Especially Prissy.

Wait, I think I hear horses. I must warn – it's Massa Andrews! I'm hidden here in the trees, but I shall document it all.

Massa is not happy. He and several other men on horseback are rounding everybody up. I can see Mama frantically looking for me. A man hits Papa.

He falls to the ground. I must go.
   May God be with us

○○ ○○ ○○ ○○ ○○

I sit in the chair, stunned. So that was where the shackles had come from. It doesn't take much of an imagination to fill in the details. Nora Mae must have put her diary back into its box before going to her family.

But if the slaves had all been shackled and taken away, why are the shackles still in the clearing? And what about the... skull... we found?

I shudder and shove the diary back into my backpack. Doesn't any story have a happy ending?

Nurse Emily comes just then. "Riley's bone marrow fluid has been thawed and prepared for use." She holds out her hand. "Mackenzie's room has a window, and the doctors have agreed to let us open the curtain. You can watch your sister receive her bone marrow." Nurse Emily leads me down the hall. An observation window in the wall looks into Mackenzie's room.

I watch as the doctors and nurses hook her up to what looks like a bag of red jam. "That's the bone marrow," Emily explains, "1500 cc's and over 45 billion cells. And thanks to your sister's drugs, her body is unable to reject it and fight it off." That sounds bad- her body is *unable* to defend itself-, but in this case, it's actually very good. Soon one of the nurses comes over and shuts the curtain again. "She needs to rest now," Nurse Emily explains.

But it has given me hope again. That bag of bone marrow is going to give life to Mackenzie.

She's going to be okay.

20

Chapter 20

Mackenzie is sick. The transplant went well. Riley is okay, other than hobbling around like an old man from soreness. The doctors had said Mackenzie was recovering quickly under the circumstances.

And then she got a fever. Her temperature skyrocketed yesterday. Her cheeks are flushed, but her body convulses with shivers. Her hand burns when I hold it.

Dr. Hobson says that fever can be one of the first signs that she's developed an infection. A stray germ might have snuck into her sterile room. In response, Dr. Hobson is increasing her antibiotics in hopes that they will ward off the infection until her new bone marrow kicks in.

Dr. Hobson lets me visit Mackenzie this morning. I stroke her forehead. Her hot skin burns through the gloves.

"Mouth's... so dry," she whispers. "Want... to go... home."

"It's okay," I soothe. "You just need to get better, then you can go home." My heart hurts like a bullet went through it, leaving a big, gaping hole. I can barely stand to see my twin sister like this. But I know she needs me more than ever, right now.

"Ride...horses. I want to visit...Oakley."

"You can ride Oakley when you're better," I say. Lauren, Mackenzie's transplant nurse, comes in and gives her another shot to help her relax. Soon Mackenzie's eyes close and her breathing deepens. I quietly leave the room.

Outside in the hall, I pull off my mask and scrubs and collapse against the wall.

"Dear God, please make my sister better," I silently plead. I let my head fall back against the wall with a thud. It hurts, but the pain barely registers. In a way, it feels good. It feels like I should have to suffer, too, if my twin sister has to go through so much pain.

I pull my head forward and let it thump back, again and again. The thought crosses my mind that I'll have a big bruise by tonight, but I don't even care. My sister is dying!

I hear footsteps running down the hall, and a man's voice yells for me to stop, but I barely hear him. A hand comes against the back of my head, cushioning it as I try to hit it against the wall.

"Stop, Taylor, Stop!" The voice finally registers, and I turn dull eyes to my dad. Tears are running down his face, and he puts his arms around me and holds me tight. I start crying, then. It's funny: I couldn't cry before, when Mackenzie first got a fever, and ever since, but now it's like the floodgates open and I can't *stop.* Dad rocks me slowly from side to side and lets me sob on his shoulder.

"Just let it all out, Taylor, " he whispers through his own tears. Finally, I'm able to stop. Dad pulls a tissue out of his pocket, and I blow my nose.

"Why her?" I finally ask him.

"I've been asking the same thing myself," Dad replies. "And we might never know why God allowed Mackenzie to be sick, and not you or I. It's the same thing I asked myself when you two came down with cancer last year. And the best answer I can come up with is that God allows these things to make us stronger, and to help us appreciate health and life a little more."

"But how can Mackenzie dying make us stronger?" I wonder, finally voicing my biggest fear to my dad. He just shakes his head.

"I don't know, baby. I don't know."

We sit there together for a while, until finally Dad gets up and says, "You better go put some ice on that head, Taylor." He never asks why or scolds me for getting the bruise. He just lets me know cares, and that's what I need most of all.

I visit Mackenzie again that afternoon. She's doing better, and not so hot or delirious.

"Did you finish... diary?" she asks me.

I avoid her gaze. "It's... not a very happy ending."

Mackenzie gives a little shrug. "Tell.. it anyway, Taylor," she insists.

"Well, Nora Mae and the rest of the slaves got caught having church in the clearing," I say slowly. "The diary ends there." I pause. Mackenzie looks at me intently.

"What happens ... next?" She whispers. I never could hide anything from her.

"Well, I researched her, then. It turns out Mr. Andrews was so mad he whipped them all almost to death, then shot them."

Mackenzie's eyes grow wide.

"Mr. Andrews was arrested the next day, though. Even in slave times you weren't allowed to just kill people."

Mackenzie gives a small smile. "I guess he got... what he.... deserved," she says softly.

I nod. "I guess so."

"Poor man," she whispers. "To live...with that kind...of hate."

I nod, amazed that my sister can so easily feel empathy for a murderer.

"What about...Tom?" she asks next.

"I looked into that, too," I say. "I didn't find anything concrete, but there is a story of a young man making it to Canada from Louisiana. He took a steamboat down the Mississippi, posing as a slave in the engine room, before following the Underground Railroad to Canada."

My sister manages another small smile. "Least…that's a good… ending," she whispers.

We both stare into space for a bit, then Mackenzie says, "Taylor, you know, I'm not afraid to die anymore. Despite how sad Nora Mae's… story is, she's in a better… place now." Mackenzie takes a few deep breaths, holding up her hand to keep me from interrupting. "I know if I die… I will be, too. So I'm not afraid."

I grip her hand. "Mackenzie, you won't die. There are good doctors here, and you have to fight, Mackenzie."

"I know…" she whispers, her voice fading, "But I'm just so… tired." Her grip loosens, and her head relaxes on the pillow. All the monitors start beeping. Her breathing is slow and shallow. I flatten myself in the corner as the doctors rush on. They aren't sterile, but at this point, it doesn't matter.

I stare at the line on the one monitor. Instead of the usual blips, it's just a straight line with the occasional erratic activity.

The sheets hit the floor. "I can't get her blood pressure!" Dr. Hobson yells.

The monitor whines instead of doing its usual, steady blip-blip. A burly nurse begins doing CPR on Mackenzie. The monitor has gone totally flatline. Lauren grabs me by the shoulder.

"You have to get out, " she tells me. "Hospital policy when they're doing CPR."

"No!" I scream. "She's my sister!"

Dr. Hobson glances at me. My knuckles are white from gripping the bed railing as Lauren tries to pry them off. He gives Lauren a quick nod, and she stops trying to pull me away.

"Okay, but you have to stand over by the wall so we can work," she says. I quickly follow her directions. It won't take much for them to kick me out of here, especially since I know the hospital policies. Family members aren't supposed to be present during CPR.

The monitor explodes into an irregular commotion of activity. The green line dances bizarrely over the screen.

"She's gone into V-fib!" someone yells. The crash cart in one corner of the room is quickly pulled over.

The burly nurse stops CPR as a flash of steel cuts through her hospital gown. I watch in horror as electrodes are slapped on her chest. Dr. Hobson sets the shock strength on the machine, and there's a whine as it ramps up. It's kind of like some of those hospital shows, but way worse.

"All clear!" someone yells out. On the bed, Mackenzie's body jerks up as the machine shocks her, hopefully getting her heart to beat again. I watch the monitor breathlessly, as the big nurse resumes CPR. There is nothing. Then a tiny blip, so fast I'm not sure if I really see it. A nurse yanks open the curtain of the observation window so the rest of the family can see Mackenzie in case this is her last moment on earth. Then another blip crosses the screen, and another. The blips get fast and tall, sometimes close together, and sometimes far apart. Finally, after a few minutes, they settle into a faint rhythm. The nurse stops CPR, and Lauren checks Mackenzie's vitals. Dr. Hobson calls for a shot of epinephrine, and gives it through an IV.

"We've got a pulse!" a nurse yells, her fingers on Mackenzie's neck.

The doctor bends over Mackenzie's still form and claps her hands.

"Mackenzie! Can you hear me?" There is no response.

"Talk to her, Taylor!" the doctor instructs. "It might not seem like it, but she can hear you!" I run to my sister's bedside. All around me, the people work feverishly, but my world has gone into slow motion. I don't realize I am crying until something wet splashes onto Mackenzie's pillow.

"Fight, Mackenzie, you have to fight!" I whisper urgently.

She opens her eyes just then. I look into the deep blue of them as she whispers, "I love you, Taylor."

"I love you, too! Please don't die on me!" I scream.

Her eyes close again, but her hand grips mine with enough strength to let me know she's still alive.

"Can you hear me?" I scream. "Wake up, Mackenzie! I need you!"

She moans, and the sound pierces my heart. Her eyelashes flutter, but stay closed.

"Blood pressures 110/60" Nurse Lauren calls out.

"Ribs are good. Nothing broken," the burly nurse notes.

"I need IV fluids going into her within the next two minutes!" Dr. Hobson calls as he administers more epinephrine.

"Blood pressures up to 120/70!" Lauren says.

I grasp Mackenzie's fingers in mine. Instead of burning up like they usually are, they feel nice and warm–just right.

"Blood oxygen is up to 96%," another nurse calls.

The green line on the monitor goes up and down in a steady rhythm.

Finally, Dr. Hobson gives her the final shot of epinephrine and steps back. "That was a close one, guys," he says, breathing hard. Mackenzie's grip on my hand tightens, and her eyes open a crack.

"Blood pressure is up to 130/80," Lauren says, removing the cuff. She continues to monitor the rest of Mackenzie's vitals while Dr. Hobson gives instructions to another nurse for a second sterile room to be prepared for Mackenzie. Activity swirls around me as they clean up, but it barely registers. I just keep staring at my sister's half closed eyes, willing her to fight through this and get better.

For a second, she opens her eyes wide and smiles at me. Then she recedes back into the dark world of a coma.

21

Chapter 21

Mackenzie is holding onto life by a thread. The doctors moved her into another sterile room as quickly as possible, but the rush into her old room to save her life brought in more deadly germs, and her infection is getting worse. The doctors had to remove fluid from her lungs earlier today, and she has developed a rash on her arms and neck. Dr. Hobson says this most likely means she has developed graft-vs-host disease- her new bone marrow is attacking her body. GVH is incurable, and Mackenzie will have to live with its effects for the rest of her life.

She's still stable, but she hasn't regained consciousness since her brush with death two days ago, and her fever has climbed back up to where it was before her heart almost stopped. No one is allowed in her new room right now besides Dr. Hobson and Lauren, so I spend most of my time at the observation window, watching the rise and fall of her chest. Thankfully this room also has a window, or I don't know what I would do.

That's where I'm standing right now, fists clenched, watching Lauren administer more antibiotics. Riley comes up behind me and puts an arm around my shoulders.

"I wish I could talk to my bone marrow, and tell it that Mackenzie is a great place for it to be, and it should fight off the infection instead of attacking her," he whispers.

I lean my head back on his shoulder. "She'll pull through it," I whisper back. "She has to."

Nurse Lauren comes out and gives us a sympathetic smile as she shrugs out of her gown and mask.

"How is she?" Riley asks.

Lauren shakes her head. "Not any better. The fluid hasn't come back on her lungs, though, so that's hopeful."

She comes over and gives me a hug. "Hang in there, Taylor," she whispers in my ear.

Inside the sterile room, something starts beeping loudly. Lauren whirls around and rushes back in. Riley and I are glued to the window. Within thirty seconds, doctors and nurses are rushing down the hall. It's just like the last time. I feel like I'm living a nightmare all over again.

From my spot by the window, I can see the heart monitor. The line has gone completely flat.

I run for the door of the room. Riley holds me back, tears streaming down his face.

"Let me go!" I scream. "Let me see my sister! She needs me!"

"You can't get in the way!" Riley yells in my ear. "The doctors need room to help her! And one more non sterile person will just increase the risk that she'll develop an infection!"

"But she's dying!" I cry. I muster every ounce of strength and break away from him. I run for the door. The knob turns from the inside as I reach for it, and I run into Lauren.

"Come in," she says, pushing me into the room. "You too, Riley."

Deep down, I know what this must mean. Lauren heads down the hall to the family room where my parents are. I just block everything from the room except for my sister, lying still on the bed. The big burly nurse from last time is doing CPR. The monitor is still completely flat line. She looks so small and pale compared to the nurse. He adjusts his position without missing a beat, so I can get closer to my sister.

"Mackenzie, please wake up!" I plead, tears running down my face. "You have to wake up! You did last time!"

But something feels different this time. It's like a heavy cloak of sadness has already descended on the room. Mom and Dad come rushing in on Lauren's heels, and we all crowd around Mackenzie's bed. Dr. Hobson nods at the nurse, and he stops CPR. Twenty minutes have passed since they first started CPR.

I don't even realize I'm clutching Mackenzie's hand until she gives it a faint squeeze. I'm about to cry out that she's responding until I look down at her chest. It isn't moving. The green line is flat.

"11:52," Dr. Hobson notes quietly. The world goes black.

oo oo oo oo oo

"Look at the stars," Dad says to six year old Mackenzie. I climb up on the deck chair and lean against the railing.

"Look down, M'kenzie. It's so far!" I squeal.

"Why can't we go up the roof like Riley?" Mackenzie pouts.

"Because Riley is older and bigger than you, and if you slip and fall, you'll get hurt really bad," Dad explains for the tenth time.

"When we're that big, we can go up, right Daddy?" I ask, also for the tenth time.

"That's right, Taylor," Dad confirms. "Right now you can see the stars just as good from the top porch."

"What's that star, Daddy?" Mackenzie asks, pointing randomly up into the sky. Dad tilts his head up.

"Hmmm, that star looks just like you, Mackenzie– bright and beautiful." Mackenzie giggles.

"Which one looks like me, Daddy?" I ask anxiously, not wanting to be left out.

"That one right beside Mackenzie's star. I think I'll have to make up a new constellation, and call it, maybe, the 'Twin Girls'."

I laugh. "You're funny, Daddy." He winks at me.

The ladder starts rattling beside us, and Mom and Riley climb down past us, and keep going all the way to the ground. I wave at them as they climb by.

"Did you see lots of stars?" Mackenzie yells over the railing."

"Same ones that you saw," Riley grunts.

Then suddenly I have a bird's eye view of the roof. Riley is lying flat on his back at the tippy-top, staring up at the sky.

"See that really bright star up there in the Little Dipper?" Riley says to himself. "That's Polaris, or the North Star. It's special, because it's really bright, and it never seems to move."

His voice seems to travel through the night, getting louder and closer to me.

"I went up here one time last summer when you two were sick. I couldn't understand why God didn't heal you guys, and why I was the healthy one." His voice stops, and I want to tell him to keep going.

"I was just staring up at the sky, talking with– okay, kind of yelling at– God," he finally continues, "and all of a sudden the North Star just jumped out at me. And this thought just went through my head that, 'God's like that star.' Sometimes He's hard to see, but He always stays the same, just like how the North Star never seems to move, and He's happy to give you direction."

Then the roof disappears into the night. The stars all swirl together into a whirling white vortex, before fading away.

My eyes slowly open. The room comes into focus. It's stark white, and the lights are too bright. Something cool and wet is lying on my head, and I reach up to pull it off.

"She's awake!" Someone calls excitedly. A nurse in pale pink scrubs hurries over. *Am I in a hospital? Do I have cancer again? What's happening?*

Then it all comes crashing down on me, like a lead weight. *I don't have cancer again. But Macknzie does-did. She's...dead.*

A moan escapes from my lips, and a woman-Mom-leans over me. I turn my head. Dad and Riley are crowded around my bedside, their eyes sad and red from crying.

"She...it's not just a dream, is it?" I ask desperately, hoping it isn't real.

Mom slowly shakes her head and sits down on the bed beside me. "She's...gone, Taylor."

"But what am I doing in a hospital bed?" I suddenly wonder. Nothing makes sense, except for the giant hole in my heart.

"You...fainted when the doctors called it. You were right beside her when she...passed away."

"I don't remember!" I say desperately, sitting up. The cold cloth on my head falls onto my lap. "Why don't I remember? My twin sister just...I can't remember!"

A panicked feeling grips me. The most traumatic thing in my life just happened and *I can't remember.* I remember rushing into the room behind the nurses after fighting Riley, and a flat green line on the monitor, but after that, it's all just blank.

"Shhh," Lauren soothes, pushing me back against the pillows. "It's okay. Sometimes when traumatic things happen, our brain blocks them out to help us not hurt so bad," she explains, "or at least that's what it's trying to do. There's nothing wrong with you, Taylor. It's okay."

"But I can't remember my last moments with her," I say, crying bitterly into the pillow. I know I was there when it happened, but I just *can't remember.*"

Riley comes over and kneels beside my bed.

"It's okay, Taylor," he says. "Mackenzie's in a better place now."

Then Mom and Dad come up beside him. I sit up in bed, and this time Lauren doesn't stop me. We all put our arms around each other and sob.

22

Chapter 22

They say October is a beautiful time of year, but all I see is the dying. The plants are dying, the trees are dying. Soon the leaves will fall.

Everything looks dreary. The dull ache inside my chest makes it hard to do anything. Mackenzie's funeral was yesterday, and she was buried in the Everett family cemetery near our plantation. The funeral memories are just a dull blur.

Riley comes outside just then, and sits beside me on the porch swing.

"You know, as hard as this is on me, I can't imagine how it is on you," he says finally. "She was your twin."

"She was like a part of me; my best friend," I answer numbly. I still can't remember her last moments, and although I've come to accept it, it still bugs me.

"I remember when Mom and Dad first brought you two home from the hospital. I didn't know Mom was having twins, or maybe they told me and I was just too young to understand, but I was so surprised to have *two* little baby sisters at one time. I thought it was the best thing ever."

"I'm sure you wished sometimes later than you only had *one* of us to deal with," I say, cracking a smile.

Riley gives a short laugh. "Maybe sometimes, but it never lasted."

We fall back into silence, and I stare numbly out across the gardens. Mom and Dad come out and join us, and we watch the trees swaying slowly in the breeze.

We sit in silence for awhile, until Mom says suddenly, "Remember the time that Taylor and Mackenzie spiced up the soup at the Ladies' Aid?"

"And that crazy wig she used to wear?" Dad adds.

"And that time that Mackenzie was convinced she could make a parachute out of a towel and she jumped off the garden shed and sprained her wrist?" Riley says.

"And I was jealous because she had a pink cast and got all these gifts, and I didn't," I say, starting to smile.

Soon we're all sharing our favorite memories of Mackenzie. We start out laughing and end up crying. Dad points to an orange leaf, dancing in the wind. "You know, Mackenzie's not really dead," he says, "she's up in Heaven, dancing, like that leaf."

"She wouldn't want us to sit around being miserable," I add, wiping my eyes, "she'd want us to live."

And as I sit there, between Riley and Dad, I know that the best way to honour her is to live my best life. The pain in my chest might dull with time- and reliving her too-short life through the pictures and memories we have helps- but I will never forget her. Every time I look in the mirror, she'll be staring back at me- brown hair, greenish gold eyes, and all. Every time I go to the stables, Oakley will be there, right beside Stormy. When I go to bed, there will be an empty one in the room, a stark reminder of what was -no, of what still is. Because Mackenzie is still very much alive, dancing on streets of gold in Heaven. And her memory lives on in our hearts.

I lie in bed that night, holding the lock of hair that I had hung on the cork board. And I know I wouldn't trade places anymore. I would have given my life to experience Mackenzie's pain while she was still here, but I wouldn't wish the sorrow I feel now on her while I got to be in heaven.

I cry into my pillow, remembering. Remembering that first day back in school in May: remembering all our pranks on our friends, remembering our adventures in the woods, and our escapades at camp. And suddenly I have this idea. I pull on a sweater and tiptoe down the stairs and outside.

The ladder is still leaning against the house out back from when we went stargazing earlier in the summer. The sky is clear and the night is still. I realize halfway up the ladder that I forgot to bring my headlamp, but the moon is bright enough that I just keep climbing.

At the top, I make my way up to the exact same spot we laid down our blankets back in July. I find the spot I think Mackenzie lay down that night, and roll onto my back. I stare up at a blanket of black velvet, sprinkled with diamond stars and a golden half moon. And that's when I remember. I'm standing beside her bedside. The nurse has stopped CPR, and the line on the monitor is flat, not a single little blip. And then she squeezes my hand. She says 'Goodbye' and 'I love you' one more time before she dies.

I blink back the tears and carefully scan the night sky, searching for it. My eyes quickly locate the Big Dipper, and I reach up and trace an imaginary line from the two pointer stars in the 'cup' to a bright star in the Little Dipper.

It's there, right where it should be, because the North Star doesn't seem to move.

"Just like You don't move, God. It's me that moves. And every time I come back, You're right where I left You. And when clouds come, stuff like grief and sadness and dying, You shine on, guiding me to where I'm supposed to go."

I imagine Mackenzie up there, looking at the *other* side of all these constellations. I imagine telling Jesus all of our adventures. And the hole in my heart doesn't feel so big anymore. It's always going to hurt, but I know I will always be grateful for our last summer together: *The Summer of Us.*

Epilogue

Next summer

About forty or so kids stood around in a semicircle, holding small, cardboard boxes tied shut with ribbons. At one end of the crowd, the camp director gave a heartfelt speech.

I clutched my box in my hand. It, like every other box, was tied shut with two ribbons. One says *Kobe* on it, and the other, *Mackenzie*, in honour of the two camp mates, friends, and siblings we have lost.

After we shared memories of the ones who have gone to Heaven, the camp director gave us the signal and we all pulled the ribbons off of our boxes. Dozens of colourful butterflies were released into the air.

I stood there, looking at the sky full of oranges and reds and pinks and greens as they fluttered away on the window. Everyone had tears in their eyes as we paid tribute to the ones we had lost, and still missed every day. I clutched the two ribbons in my hand and watched the horizon until the last butterfly faded from sight.

Does it still hurt? Yes. But I have hope, that healing will come, and God can use this for His good.

Afterword

First and foremost, thank you God, for giving me the ideas and abilities to tell this story. May the glory always be Yours.

I also owe a thank you to the following people:

- Lois Bowman, for typing out the original manuscript and giving me that first push towards publishing.
- My family, especially my Mom, for proofreading my manuscript and helping me edit it.
- All the helpful people at Reedsy. Rodney H., your advice about self-publishing helped me greatly.
- My cover artist and designer, Steve K. You helped me bring my ideas to life.
- My special friends and cousins; my biggest fans and cheerleaders. If you don't know who you are, you can come ask me ;)